COLORADO BLOOD HUNT

Heading towards the Colorado town of Hope to seal a cattle purchase deal, Jess McCall rides straight into trouble when a man erupts from the bush in front of him, screaming in pain — and burning alive. When attempting to help, McCall is ambushed by a trio who knock him out and truss him up, intending to carry him into town and name him as the man's murderer. But his attackers have underestimated their victim. McCall won't stay down easily . . .

NEIL HUNTER

COLORADO BLOOD HUNT

Complete and Unabridged

LINFORD
Leicester

First published in Great Britain in 2016

First Linford Edition
published 2017

A catalogue record for this book is available
from the British Library.

ISBN 978–1–4448–3341–6

Published by
F. A. Thorpe (Publishing)
Anstey, Leicestershire

Set by Words & Graphics Ltd.
Anstey, Leicestershire
Printed and bound in Great Britain by
T. J. International Ltd., Padstow, Cornwall

This book is printed on acid-free paper

1

Jess McCall hung onto the single thought lodged stubbornly in his mind. *At least they ain't killed you yet, son.* And while he was still able to breathe he figured he had a chance. So thin as to be transparent, but a chance. His body was aching from being dragged behind a horse and his clothes were starting to shred. There was an egg-sized lump on the back of his skull where one of his captors had whacked him with his pistol, blood streaking his face from being hit, and one idiot was still cackling like an old woman as he went on about how he was considering stringing McCall up and making sure he was dead before they hauled him into town.

McCall's forward motion stopped. He cracked one eye and looked around. From where he lay he could see the three horses belonging to the men who

1

had brought him down and dragged him.

He tried to make sense of the whole damned thing. It wasn't easy. Bouncing and rolling on the end of that rope had shaken his senses until coherent thought was difficult. He forced himself to concentrate, ignoring the pain and fought to recall how it had all started . . .

Then it came back to him.

The burning man.

That was where it started.

A screaming, writhing human form thrashing around on the ground in front of McCall. One minute he had been moving through the Colorado high country, minding his own business as he headed through the timbered slopes, admitting that it was a nice place for a quiet ride. A good day, with the sun slanting through the timber. The air fresh and clean. The brush was thick and green. He could see why anyone would settle here. It was big, spacious, and quiet.

That was until the burning man erupted from the brush just ahead of

McCall. He was on fire from head to foot, his body enveloped in flame that ate at his flesh and clothing. For a moment McCall was frozen at the sight as the figure stumbled and crashed to the ground, rolling and squirming as he tried vainly to extinguish the fire. The sound coming from his throat was unnerving. It didn't even sound human. A sound of pure terror ripped from the man's very being.

Snapping out of the moment McCall dropped from his horse and yanked at his blanket roll, freeing it from the strings holding it together. He shook it out, moving towards the burning man. He wasn't even sure if he could do any good but he also knew he had to do something.

He had barely reached the man when he sensed he wasn't alone any longer. A quick glance and he saw three riders. They came boiling out of the brush, the leader a youngish man with a wild grin on his face. The ones behind him hard-looking as they crowded the lead rider.

'Mister, he don't need that blanket,' the man said, his grin widening. 'Seems to me he's warm enough.' He burst into laughter, the sound high and shrill.

McCall ignored him and swung his blanket, ready to drop it over the man on the ground.

'*I said leave him.*' The young man waved a hand at one of his partners. 'Buck, convince him.'

The one called Buck had already reached for the rope on his saddle. He uncoiled it with a practised wrist and formed a loop. He pushed his horse forward, swinging the rawhide rope in McCall's direction. McCall saw the loop dropping towards him and pulled back, letting go the blanket. He was too late. The loop dropped over his shoulders and tightened as the man called Buck snubbed his rope around his saddle horn and gigged his horse back. McCall felt the loop tighten, pinning his arms to his side. He lost his balance and went down, landing hard enough to knock his breath from his body.

4

McCall felt himself being dragged forward, unable to even reach for his holstered Colt. The rope was kept taut and he knew he wasn't going to free it anytime soon.

'Get this *hombre* on his feet.'

The third rider dismounted and stepped over McCall. He was a big man, wide-shouldered, hair down around his collar and a straggling mustache adorning his upper lip. His expression was sullen as he kicked the Texan in his ribs. He reached down and pulled McCall's Colt from its holster, tucking it behind his belt. Then he took hold of McCall's shoulder and hauled him upright. No mean feat because McCall was six foot six and solid built.

'All yours, Perry,' the man said.

Perry had stepped down, a long-barreled Henry rifle in his hand. He was still grinning as he faced McCall.

'Well, boys, looks like we got our killer here,' said. 'Caught in the act. Standing over poor Sturdevant and watching him burn.'

'You know that's a damn lie,' McCall said, understanding what was happening here.

'Three against one,' Perry said. 'That's the way it is, boy.'

The roper, Meers, leaned forward to spit tobacco juice. 'Way I see it, Mister Culhane, why there we were riding peaceful like and we come across this feller attacking poor old Sturdevant. Lucky we showed up when we did.'

'You see that too, Flag?'

'Sure did.'

'There you go,' Perry said. 'We got you, mister, and that's how it'll go when we haul your carcass to town.'

'Son, you got to get me there first.'

'Roped. No gun. Seems to me things aren't going your way.'

The hell they aren't, McCall decided, and without another thought he hauled off and kicked Perry hard between the legs. There was considerable force in the kick. Perry let out a high squeal, stumbling back. He dropped his rifle, both hands to his groin as he sank to his knees in pure agony.

The moment he delivered the blow McCall knew he was about to pay for it, so he derived all the satisfaction he could from seeing Perry in real pain.

Behind him, Flag snatched his pistol from its holster and used it to club the back of McCall's skull, driving him down. Dazed by the solid blow McCall decided not to offer any more resistance. Even so that failed to prevent Perry, staggering upright, bunching his fists and punching McCall in the face a couple of times. Blood welled from split lips, spilling down McCall's chin. He felt more coming from a gash in his cheek and from one over his left eye.

Well, son, you at least got in one good shot.

Knowing that didn't make him feel any more comfortable.

McCall wasn't aware of falling face down. Everything got hazy then. When he cleared his mind as much as he could he realized he had his wrists roped and he was being dragged along behind one of the horses and managed to wonder if the day could get any worse.

Unfortunately for McCall it *could* and it *did*.

2

Perry Culhane.

McCall would remember that name even if everything else got lost. He lay still, watching as they dismounted and stood together, having some kind of discussion. It was obvious Culhane was top dog. He acted and spoke like he was used to being in charge and the two others, Meers and Flag, were subordinates. Despite his uncomfortable condition McCall at least enjoyed seeing that Culhane was still suffering from the kick he had administered. The man moved slowly, slightly hunched over, and that at least brought a little sunshine into McCall's otherwise bad day.

Flag broke out stuff from his possibles sack. While he did this Meers gathered wood for a cookfire. It appeared they were in no hurry to keep moving. Culhane took out a tobacco pouch and rolled himself a quirley. Lit it with a burning twig from the cook fire and leaned his back against a tree.

McCall picked up the sound of fast moving water and when he slowly turned his head he saw a wide creek behind the trees where Culhane was standing. He kept that in mind. He was searching for a possible escape route. When his chance came — when not if — McCall would take it. It made sense to him. He had no intention of sitting back and allowing his fate to be decided by someone else. Especially by the three fellers who had him momentarily at a disadvantage.

Jess McCall was not the kind to meekly sit back and simply bemoan his bad luck. He didn't have that kind of outlook. Which meant this Texas boy would find a way to get himself out this mess and bring misfortune to the simple sons who were figuring they had it all worked out. They would learn the error of their ways soon enough. McCall had been looking out for himself since his

10

teenage years. That was the way it was on the Texas frontier. It was not a place for the tender hearted, or shrinking violets. A man had to stand on his own two feet and smite the other feller before he got himself smitten. Easy going in most circumstances Jess McCall could change quickly, and when that happened a Texas twister had nothing on Mrs. McCall's boy.

So while he studied the situation and worked on his escape McCall stayed quiet and still, not wanting to warn Perry Culhane and company what was going to come down on them when he made his move.

In time Flag cooked a meal. McCall admitted the smell of frying bacon and hot coffee was tempting, though he doubted his hosts were going to offer him any. He watched as they helped themselves and hunkered down around the fire.

If you're going to do something, son, now is the time.

He had been gradually working on

the rope around his wrists. The rawhide had chafed his skin, making it bleed and if anything that helped. The blood softened the rawhide. Not by much yet enough for McCall to work at it. When the taut loops around his wrists suddenly slackened McCall stilled his actions. He glanced at the three men around the cookfire and picked up their talk.

★ ★ ★

' . . . that damn Indian girl,' Flag said harshly. 'Her running off like she done. What if she talks to someone?'

'*Who?*' That was Perry himself. 'Way out here who the hell is she goin' to find? A squaw. And I hit her pretty hard. She ain't in no condition to stay on her feet long.'

'Ain't as if we got time to go searching for her,' Meers said. 'Not in these hills. She could be anywhere.'

'With a piece of luck she'll fall off some drop and break her neck,' Perry said.

'Easy to say,' Flag said. 'What if she don't? What if she shows up in town?'

'On foot? All that way and hurtin' the way she is? Ty, we got the only feller who saw us with Sturdevant and once we drag him to town and tell our story he ain't going to have much luck on his side.'

'I'm not so damn sure,' Flag grumbled.

'Jesus, you're like some old woman. Look, ain't no one in town to stand up against me.' He jerked a thumb over his shoulder. 'We got the one who done it. We point the finger he's got no chance.'

*   *   *

While this discussion was going on McCall worked on his tied wrists, and after a few minutes, stretching the loops until he was able to slip his hands free he checked to see his captors were still relaxed as they talked over how they were going to drag him to town. He coiled the rope around him again in case one of them decided to take a look in his direction. He could feel the circulation returning to his hands, realizing he needed that to complete before he made any moves.

The trio were obviously in no great hurry to carry on with their ride. McCall hoped that situation lasted. He took stock. Their three horses were tethered to a handy tree, with his own mount alongside. Making a run for his horse was not an sensible option. Even if he reached his mount he had to loosen the reins before he could get into the saddle and ride off. Even the slowest gunhand would have the time to get off a shot during that time.

The creek was the best chance he had. If he could get into the water the flow would carry him away at a pretty fast rate. The idea sounded fine. The trouble was he had no idea what conditions he might find once he was in that water. Hidden rocks. Rapids. McCall dismissed the negative thoughts. Anything was better than remaining in the hands of the three miserable honchos who were bound and determined to put the blame for the death of the man called Sturdevant onto Jess McCall.

He wondered briefly how it was a man's luck could change so damned quickly. From a peaceable ride minding his own business, to being trussed up and dragged by men he hadn't known existed with the promise of even more misery being piled on him. McCall didn't spend too much thought on that. It had happened so all he needed to concentrate on was getting himself out this jam and to hell with anyone who got hurt in the process.

His chance came when Meers stood and turned to go to the horses, where he opened a saddle bag and began rooting around for something. It took him away from the others, most likely only for a short time, but that was all McCall needed. As he tensed, ready to push to his feet, McCall saw Perry Culhane stand too, stretching his lean body to ease out the kinks from sitting.

The man had his back to McCall. So McCall came to his own feet, pushing hard and broke into a run, ignoring the protest from his battered body.

He covered the distance fast and came up behind the still seated Flag just as the man sensed McCall's presence. Flag started to come upright, snatching for the pistol on his right hip, a yell forming on his lips. McCall hit him full on, the Texan's weight slamming into Flag. The impact spun Flag off his feet and he fell face down across the cookfire, his yell turning into a scream of pain as he squirmed and wriggled, pawing at the burning embers searing into his flesh. McCall kept right on moving, his big right fist swinging as he came face-to-face with Perry Culhane. It thumped Culhane across the jaw, jerking his head around in a blur. Culhane fell back, stunned, blood forming on his lips. He stumbled to his knees. McCall paused for a fraction, snatching Culhane's pistol from his holster, then kept moving, through the stand of trees that edged the bank of the creek.

McCall caught a glimpse of the choppy brown water an instant before he went over the bank and into the creek. He sank immediately, managing to close his mouth before the icy water closed over his head and he felt the fierce grip of the current as it grabbed him and dragged him along. McCall didn't fight the pull of the water. He let it take him. He managed to get his head clear and keep a grip on the pistol he had taken from Culhane.

It seemed an age before McCall picked up on the sound of shots. A couple came close, slapping the water only feet away. Then the creek took a wide turn and he was out of sight. McCall was rolled and turned, his body held in the grip of the water. More than once his head went under and he had to be certain to keep his mouth closed each time it happened.

He felt the flow of the water increase. Moving faster. It became overpowering and now he was struggling to keep his head above the surface. It didn't take him long to figure out why. The churning water started to show white foam as it bounded ahead of him and McCall heard a deep roaring sound. He understood what that meant.

Rapids.

The creek was dropping over a fall.

He made an abortive attempt to swim to the side. It was pointless. The strength of the fast flowing water was too much for him and before he knew it he was flung over the drop. He was lost in the mass of water. Was turned over and twisted from side to side. Gasping for air he hit the bottom of the fall and by some miracle his head broke the surface as the water carried him forward. McCall greedily sucked in precious air. As he was swept away from the fall the flow of the creek lessened and McCall found he was able to reach the bank. It was hard to drag himself out of the water where he lay on the slight incline.

He had no idea how long he lay stretched out on the creek bank, the warm sun on his back. McCall became aware of something in his right hand and when he managed to turn his aching head he saw he was still clutching the Colt he had snatched from Perry Culhane's holster.

'Son of a bitch,' he muttered. 'You were like to drown but you didn't let go that damn smoke wagon.' He managed a slow chuckle. 'Always look after the important things in life.'

It penetrated McCall's brain that Culhane and his partners might be searching for him. So laying around on the ground might not be the wisest way to see out the day. He pulled himself into a sitting position, which reminded him how much abuse he had already suffered. He figured Culhane might be aggrieved to a degree because McCall had managed to break away. The thing was just how *much* Culhane might be angry. McCall didn't know him all that well, but from their short time together he decided Perry Culhane was the kind who would hold a grudge. It was plain to see the man liked his own willful way and would not be inclined to back off. Not especially when there was a witness to something he and his partners had done.

'Hell, Jess,' he said, 'I thought it was going to be a nice day.'

He stood, arching his aching body. Searching for a way to go that would take him away from Culhane and company. Choosing his path McCall set off, shaking the Colt in his hand to shed the water that had got inside. He worked out the .45 caliber bullets and wondered how badly they might have been soaked during his trip down the creek. The same went for the shells in his own belt loops. His curiosity got the better of him and he inspected Perry Culhane's weapon. It was a nice piece of ordnance. Nickel-plated with ivory grips. Each grip had the letters *P* and *C* engraved on them. McCall wondered if it was a working gun, or simply one for show. He couldn't see Culhane as a skilled gun. But he could be wrong. Maybe he was doing the man an injustice. Not that he wouldn't enjoy doing that if the chance showed up.

He walked for close on an hour, working his way up a long, timbered slope until he was able to look back over the ground he had covered. It was difficult to see anything because of the close timber. He located the creek and followed it back as far as he could. The water glittered in fragments through the trees and brush.

Then he saw them.

Three riders breaking from the trees into a clear section. His own horse was still with them, one of the riders leading it by its reins. They were still a way off. Being on horseback meant they could cover more ground than McCall.

He was still considering that when a distant shout reached his ears. One of the distant riders had swung up the rifle in his hands. McCall saw the puff of smoke. The slug chunked into the slope a few feet to his left, the sound of the shot reaching him a moment later.

They had him spotted.

McCall sighed. More in resignation than anything else. Whatever else Culhane and his partners might be, they were persistent. He watched them as they spurred their horses towards the base of the slope. He reached down and drew the Colt, weighing it in his hands. Maybe a warning shot would give them pause. He aimed the pistol at the ground ahead of them. Eased back the hammer and pulled the trigger. The hammer dropped and all McCall heard was the solid click as it struck the cartridge. His concern about water-soaked ammunition was proving correct. McCall cocked and fired again, until he had gone through the six .45 caliber loads. He leaned back out of sight and shed the bullets, replacing them with loads from his own belt loops. He began to cycle through the cylinder. He was surprised himself when the third bullet fired. He saw it strike well ahead of the lead horse.

'McCall, your luck's holding,' he said.

The gout of dirt from the slug caused the three riders to rein back. McCall knew it wouldn't be for long. He broke cover and pushed on up the slope, trying to keep the trees as cover. He had gone less than twenty feet when a shot scored a hit in a tree he was passing. Bark flew, exposing the white wood beneath. Someone was getting his range now and that meant his streak of luck was thinner than he had expected.

As he moved he thumbed a fresh cartridge into the Colt and wondered if he was going to have any more live shots. It only took one dry shell and a well-aimed shot to change the balance. The Texan also knew he was going to need his target a damn sight closer. The Colt was no match for a long gun range wise. He couldn't stop himself thinking about his own Winchester, nestling in the scabbard on his own horse.

A sudden, concentrated burst of firing shattered the silence of the forested slopes. McCall heard the hammer of slugs peppering the timber around him. He recalled his thought about all it taking was a single shot to change things. That also applied to Culhane and company — and they had more guns.

Now he could hear the sounds of thudding hooves as his pursuers gained on him. McCall didn't waste time looking behind. He simply kept moving. He had no other choices apart from giving up, and that was not going to happen.

One of the advancing horses came even closer. He picked up the sound of hooves. The creak and jingle of harness and the gusting of the animal's breathing.

McCall sensed the imminent closeness of the rider. Heard the crackling as the horse barreled its way through the brush. A shot fired. The slug burning across McCall's left side. More of a graze than a solid hit, but the pain galvanized McCall.

He pulled himself to a dead stop, raising the Colt as the bulk of rider and horse loomed large. He recognized the man called Flag, his face scorched by his fall into the cookfire, his shirt burned as well. McCall triggered a shot and the hammer fell on yet another useless cartridge. In sheer desperation McCall held back the trigger and worked the hammer with his left hand. More dead clicks, then the crash of a single shot. Flag slipped back in his saddle, a burst of red flying from his right shoulder as the .45 caliber slug hit. He forgot about his rifle, clutching his wound, and McCall moved faster than he expected himself. His big hands reached up and caught hold of Flag's arm, yanking the man from the saddle. As Flag's bulk dropped McCall jammed the Colt back into his holster, already reaching with his left hand for the saddle horn. He gathered his strength and hauled himself up across the horse as it plunged on by him, the animal's forward movement helping to boost McCall's effort.

He managed to swing his right leg over the saddle, clamping his free hand on the horse's flying mane, and fumbled his right boot into the empty stirrup as the mount carried him up the timbered slope. He lay across the saddle in an undignified sprawl but made no effort to right himself. Keeping low would make him a smaller target while he gained some distance from his pursuers and right then it was all McCall required.

Apart from staying alive.

3

The horse under McCall, a strong dark gray, surged forward under his urging and for whatever reason it increased its speed. The animal moved effortlessly up the slope, swerving back and forth to avoid the close-ranked trees, crashing through the undergrowth and taking itself and its rider further and further away from pursuit. McCall didn't check the horse's flight. He was simply grateful to be out of range of Culhane and company's guns. There was no way of telling how long the situation might last so he kept riding and made no attempt to slow the horse until it reached the uppermost slope and came to a relatively level grassy meadow.

He hauled in on the reins, bringing the panting horse to a halt. He could feel its sides heaving, hear the blow of air from its nostrils as it stood head down. McCall leaned forward and patted its neck.

'Did us proud there, son.'

He stepped from the saddle and leaned against the horse, easing the aches from his body. It had turned into one hell of a day. Dragged. Kicked. Half-drowned and shot at — he felt the sting of the bullet burn now and put his hand over the spot. Felt a sticky smear of blood. The slug had burned a small furrow across his ribs, luckily not deep and there was little blood.

The thought of the bullet wound made him think of ammunition and he moved to the saddlebags strapped behind the saddle. He went through the pouches. And pulled out a couple of boxes of cartridges. One for .44-40 caliber. For Flag's rifle, which he hadn't got. The other box held .45 caliber shells. McCall shucked the empty hulls from the Colt and replaced them with fresh ones. Holding a fully loaded weapon in his hand gave McCall a feeling of satisfaction. He plucked out the loads from his belt loops and fed fresh ones in their place. He dropped the cartridges from his belt into one of the saddlebag pouches, figuring they might dry out.

He found some strips of beef jerky wrapped in greased paper. McCall took one to chew on. He found a canteen draped from the saddelhorn. The water was warm but McCall wasn't about to complain about that. The gray must have smelled the water. It turned its head and stared at McCall.

'Don't give me that look,' McCall said. 'I lost my damn hat else I'd give you some.'

The animal continued to watch him until McCall tipped water into his palm and wet the gray's mouth. He repeated the action. It was the best he could do for now.

'Soon as we find water you can sup all you want, son. Right now this is it.' The gray shook its head, nickering softly. McCall stroked its neck. 'Time to move, feller. I don't think we're in the clear yet.'

Back in the saddle McCall turned the gray around. Back down the long slope he picked out the three riders. They were still coming on, negotiating the way. A fair way behind him, yet their determined movement told McCall they were not going to quit. A taut smile crossed his bruised, bloody face.

'Well, we got that in common,' he said quietly, ''cause I don't give up either and somewhere along the track, you boys and me got us a grievance to clear up.'

He pulled on the reins, dug in his heels and set the gray on across the wide meadow. When McCall had been travelling earlier he had been riding in a westerly direction, so he picked up his way. Somewhere to the west lay his destination and Culhane apart that was where Jess McCall was going.

Colorado.

The town of Hope.

A meeting with a man called Brigham Tyler.

The reason for McCall's presence in

Colorado was to complete the purchase of breeding cattle for the Conway Lazy-C ranch back in Texas. Henry Conway had agreed to the buy, wanting to introduce the prize beeves to his own herds. McCall had put himself forward for the trip and that was the reason for his presence here in the high country of Colorado. It was only due to a rail derailment of the train just after it had crossed from New Mexico that had put McCall in the saddle earlier than anticipated. His horse was in the box car at the rear of the train, so McCall, not eager to sit out the long wait for a repair crew to arrive, had chosen to complete his journey by horse. The thought of riding the last miles to Hope, through some of the prettiest country he had seen for a long time, appealed to him. The town lay some forty-odd miles away, which was no problem as far as McCall was concerned. The high country was green and lush. McCall was ready for some fresh air away from the confines of the train and his horse had appreciated being freed from the swaying freight car.

The first couple of hours had passed without incident and McCall, resting easy in the saddle, let his mount pick its own pace as they passed through the timbered landscape. There had been no rush and McCall had taken advantage of the leisurely trip.

McCall had carried with him an introductory letter from Henry Conway that now was in his saddlebags and the saddlebags were on his horse now being ridden by one of Perry Culhane's partners. Luckily he was not carrying anything more valuable than his personal belongings in the bags. If the purchase of the cattle was agreed, Henry Conway would transfer the asking price from his bank to Brigham Tyler's in Hope. It was, McCall decided, a good thing, because if he had lost Conway's money he would have felt a damn sight more aggrieved than he already was.

Right now even that was a minor irritation compared to his current situation. A persistent thought pushed its way into his consciousness.

It had to do with the burning man.

Who was he and what had he done to suffer the way he had?

All he had was a name — Sturdevant.

And who was this Indian girl Perry and the others had been talking about?

For a moment McCall relived the moment he had first laid eyes on the shrieking, flame-cocooned man. The shocking appearance had caught him off guard. McCall had reacted as swiftly as possible, making an attempt to help the unfortunate man, yet even that had been thwarted by the presence of Culhane and his two sidekicks. Their callous attitude had been added to by their turning on McCall when he tried to go to the burning man's aid. After that McCall had little opportunity to control the situation until the hoorawing had stopped and he was able to break free from the rope . . .

McCall had questions. Getting any answers didn't seem to be the easy thing considering he was — in loose terms — on the run in unfamiliar territory. Knowing that didn't depress McCall. Very little did. His philosophy was *if he had a problem he solved it*. Not always an easy option but Jess McCall held to it.

So right now, being chased by a hard crew, he needed to stay sharp and try to figure out the why. The big question. The one he was not going to get cleared up while he was riding these empty hills.

McCall reached a ridge overlooking a wide valley. Nestling in the floor of the valley he saw a collection of buildings with a trail leading in and out. There was the sparkle of water from a meandering creek that appeared to come from higher up the mountain slopes. The drift of smoke from chimneys told McCall the place was inhabited. It wasn't Hope because McCall had been moving in the opposite direction. He picked out the gleam of a rail line that ran past the place. It was at least a town and it offered McCall the chance, maybe small he admitted, of finding some kind of law. A Sheriff. Maybe a Marshal. His chance to tell his story. To hopefully find out who the burning man had been.

He put his horse on the downslope, closing the distance. McCall kept checking his back trail. He hadn't forgotten the three riders and he was pretty sure they hadn't forgotten about him.

There was a single street, buildings on either side. Businesses on each side. He passed a livery and corrals on the edge of town. An eating house. Dry goods store. Couple of saloons.

McCall felt a sense of unease when he realized the few people he was riding by were stopping to stare. He realized he must look a sight. Bruised and battered. His clothes wrinkled and grubby. Blood dried on his face. A man pointed. Said something to his companion, then turned and hurried off along the board-walk. The unease became stronger as other faces spread out at him.

It was only then McCall's unease manifested itself into something tangible as he took note of the sign over the saloon he was passing.

The Culhane House.

He turned in the saddle and scanned other signs.

Culhane Mercantile.

The Culhane Eatery.

Culhane Bank and Loan.

The name stood out on the majority of facings along the street.

McCall sighed.

'This just ain't your day, son,' he said to no one in particular.

He saw the man who had pointed in his direction before running off was back. Behind him was a thick-set man, wearing a heavy mustache that hung over his mouth. His face was lean and narrow. He had a badge pinned to his vest and a double-barreled shotgun he aimed at McCall.

'Show me your hands, mister, and be quick about it,' the lawman said. 'If you don't I'm about to drop you out that saddle.'

4

The man who had run to fetch the lawman was pointing at the horse McCall was sitting on.

'There, you see it, Mort. That's a Boxed-C horse. One belonging to Major Culhane. I'd say this feller is nothing but a horse thief 'cause he isn't one of the Culhane riders.'

Mort stepped closer, running his eyes over McCall's disheveled appearance. There was a look in the man's eyes that warned the Texan to step carefully with the man. McCall didn't like the way Mort was fingering the shotgun.

'Mister, you'd better step out of that saddle and have one hell of a good story to tell.'

'You just point that scatter gun away from me, son, and I'll oblige you.'

'I don't think you got much say in the matter.'

'You tell him, Mort, an' don't take any bad mouth from him.'

McCall glanced at the speaker. The man who had brought the lawman. Skinny as a rake, his pale face flushed with excitement. Dressed in a dark suit, high-collared shirt and black tie. He was figuring he was someone really important the way he crowded the deputy and kept jabbing a finger at the Texan.

'Something seems to be stuck in your craw, friend,' McCall said. 'Way you're jabbering I can see you running off to fetch a hang rope any time soon.'

The man turned his gaze on McCall. 'Wait 'til the Major finds out,' he said, his voice thin and peevish. 'He'll know what to do with you.'

McCall gave a slow smile. 'Son, I hear you, but all I see is feller who tags along in another man's shadow.'

Mort gave a harsh laugh. 'He got you there, Begley.'

Begley's thin face flushed deeply. He took a slight step back. Almost immediately he paused, stared, then gave an excited cry.

'There,' he crowed. 'In his holster . . . it's Perry's gun. *He's got Perry Culhane's gun.*'

This time even Mort showed interest, following Begley's accusing finger. The expression on his boney face hardened.

'By God, you're right. I'd recognize that fancy piece of hardware anyhows.' The shotgun centered on McCall. 'Step down, mister and do it right quick. No more playing innocent. We got you dead to rights.'

McCall saw no profit in putting up any form of resistance. Especially not with a twelve-gauge no more than a couple of feet from him. He eased himself out of the saddle, hands held well clear of his body and stood next to the horse.

'Begley, go lift that smoke wagon out his holster and bring it here,' Mort said.

For a second Begley's face dropped a shade paler than it had been originally. It was plain he was big on words but not so when it came to actions. He edged off the boardwalk and approached McCall with the expectations of a man face-to-face with a rattler.

'Y — you make sure he isn't going to make a grab for me,' he said.

'Christ, Ira, I got a head buster on him so he ain't doin' a damn thing. Now get that gun.'

McCall stood motionless, with no intention of doing anything for the moment. Resistance was a losing hand right there and then. He felt the ivory-handled revolver lifted from his holster, Begley jerking away rom him the moment he had the weapon in his hand. He scampered back onto the boardwalk, then turned to face McCall, a satisfied smirk on his face now he was out of reach.

'Perry's gun. No doubt on that,' he crowed. 'Jesus, Mort, you think he done killed Parry?'

McCall was about to make a comment but chose to remain silent. It was, he figured, the time to stay silent and see what was in the wind. He realized he had ridden into the wrong town. It appeared to favor the name of Culhane. He wasn't about to be offered much in the way of sympathy, so keeping his mouth closed looked to be a wise move for the moment.

'Let's move, mister,' Mort said, gesturing with his shotgun. 'Jail's along the street.'

He stepped off the boardwalk, close behind McCall. The shotgun centered on McCall's spine. Ira Begley fell in step next to Mort, self-importantly brandishing the retrieved Colt.

McCall caught sight of the jail. It looked to be the only stone-built building in town. Solid and with a sturdy wood door, barred windows on either side. When they reached it, under the curious gaze of other citizens, Mort prodded McCall with the shotgun.

'Keep goin'.'

What happened next did little to improve McCall's mood.

Ira Begley edged in close and hit McCall across the side of the head with the pistol in his hand.

'You heard the deputy, you son of a bitch, so step up there fast.'

McCall absorbed the sharp streak of pain from the blow, teeth clenched as he climbed to the boardwalk. He felt a worm of blood slide down the side of his face and promised himself he wasn't about to forget Mister Ira Begley in a hurry.

'Open the door, Ira,' Mort said.

Begley edged around McCall and lifted the iron latch, pushing the door wide. For a moment he was caught between the door and McCall. Despite the gun in his hand the man showed fear in his eyes, quickly stepping away from the towering figure.

As McCall walked inside he took in the scene. A typical law office. With all the usual features McCall had seen before. Sometimes on the right side of the law, sometimes not. Across the room was a barred door leading to the cell area. On his left a desk. Gun rack behind it holding an assortment of rifles and shotguns. Flyers pinned to the cork board on the wall. Stove on the other side of the office. Couple of ladder-back wooden chairs facing the desk. Windows on either side of the door with latched-back wood shutters.

Behind the desk, seated in a leather-cushioned swivel chair was the man McCall was to know as John Teague — the badge on his blue shirt indicating he was town marshal. Teague was in his forties, hair and mustache already gray. Mid-height, with wide shoulders. A competent-looking man with a searching expression in his keen eyes. His solid gaze took in McCall's condition and was not slow in seeing the fresh trickle of blood coming from the gash in the side of his head.

'Somebody like to tell me what's going on?'

'This man rode into town on a Boxed-C horse,' Begley said in a rush. 'And he had Perry Culhane's gun. We caught him. Figured he's smart but we caught him.'

Teague's uncompromising stare moved

from Begley to his deputy. In that brief moment McCall saw something like distaste in his expression.

The marshal doesn't take to Begley, he thought. *Could be in my favor.*

'Mort?'

'True enough,' Mort said. 'Rode in big as all get out on a Boxed-C nag. Had Perry's gun in his holster.'

Teague considered the words, then glanced at McCall.

'What happened out there?' he asked.

'We braced him and brought him in,' Mort said.

'He resist?'

'No. I had my shotgun on him.'

'He fall down?'

Mort's confusion was all too obvious. 'No.'

'So how did he get that fresh cut on his head? Still bleeding.'

Even McCall felt the silence that fell over the room. He decided it was his turn to say something.

'That came from the other *deputy*,' he said quietly. 'The one who must have forgot to pin on his badge this morning.'

Mort kind of cleared his throat as Teague fixed Begley with an unwavering look.

'Ira, put the gun on my desk.'

Begley did what he was asked.

'*He* . . . ' His voice was low, shaky. 'This man . . . '

'Door's behind you, Begley. I suggest you use it before I decide I ought to charge you with assault.'

'The Major won't be pleased about this.'

'Now that will give me no sleepless nights. Just get out of my sight. Go scuttle off and tell Major Culhane you're lucky I'm not tossing you into one of those cells back yonder. *Now get out.*'

Begley left without another word, closing the office door.

'Mort put down the shotgun. Take the horse this man rode in on to the stable and tend to it. Then do your rounds. And, Mort, take your time.'

'What about him?'

'I can handle . . . mister?'

'McCall. Jess McCall.'

'We'll be fine, Mort. You go do what I just told you.'

'You're the boss,' Mort said.

'That I am, Mort. It's just nice to be reminded once in a while.'

Mort exited the office, leaving McCall and Teague alone.

'Sit down, McCall. I imagine we got some talking to do.'

McCall dropped into one of the chairs. He heard Teague moving about behind him. When he reappeared he handed McCall a folded cloth and a tin basin of warm water. McCall used it to clean the gash in his head. A mug of coffee was placed on the desk in front of McCall, then Teague returned to his own seat.

'You got something to tell me, Mister McCall?'

McCall told him, relating everything that had happened from the moment he had been confronted by the burning man. He told it straight, with no embellishments, hiding nothing and when he'd finished Teague leaned back in his seat, showing nothing on his face. He drew a big hand across his mouth, nodding slowly as he absorbed McCall's story.

McCall devoted his time to drinking the coffee which was welcome following his journey to town.

'I have two choices,' Teague said. 'One I figure you're a damn good story teller and the other is that you've told me the truth.'

'Can I make a suggestion, Marshal?'

'Sure.'

'Send a couple of telegraph messages. One to Marshal Ray Bellingham in Beecher's Crossing, Texas. The other to Brigham Tyler of Hope, Colorado. Ask them who I am and if they'll vouch for me.'

'You're way ahead of me there,' Teague said. 'That's just what I'm about to do.'

Teague got to his feet, picking up a

bunch of keys. McCall understood what was going to happen. He drained his coffee and showed the mug to Teague.

'Mind if I take another mug with me?'

Teague refilled the mug. He handed it to McCall and followed him through to the cells in back of the jail.

'I hope you'll take this as just a precaution,' he said as he locked McCall into one of the empty cells. 'I know you ain't been charged with anything but I'd not be doing my job if I didn't hold you for now.'

McCall sat on the edge of the cot. 'Be obliged if you could send me in some food. Right now I'm hungry.'

'Leave it with me.'

'Marshal. Just one thing.'

'Ask it.'

'I have a feeling I already know the answer, but humor me. What's the name of this town?'

A smile ghosted across Teague's face. '*Culhane*,' he said. 'Like most everything else the Major owns.'

He picked up on McCall's unwavering look.

'No, McCall, he doesn't own *me*.'

McCall raised his coffee mug. 'I should have guessed.'

'McCall, you brought me a mess of questions that need answering, so sit tight while I earn my pay.'

'I reckon the answer to one of those questions is something we both need to know.'

Teague nodded.

'*Who was the man on fire?* That, McCall, is top of my list.'

'All I got was the name Sturdevant. That mean anything?'

'Yes it does.'

5

Brigham Tyler was already in Hope, waiting for Jess McCall to show up. He sat in his brother Seth's office in Hope's jail and already carried a feeling of concern over McCall's lateness. The train McCall had been on had finally showed up hours behind schedule and when Brig had made inquiries he had been told that McCall had decided to leave the train and ride the last leg of the journey to town. Yet he hadn't shown up and it was well past the expected time. Brigham Tyler had never met McCall, but from the telegrams sent between Hope and Beecher's Crossing he had been told that Jess McCall was a dependable man, not given to tardiness.

'You think he might have got off track?' Seth asked.

Brigham shook his head. 'Feeling I

get from Henry Conway is McCall is too good a man to lose himself.'

Being the Marshal of Hope allowed Seth Tyler to look beyond what might be expected of someone. He pushed up out of his chair and came around the desk and examined the map pinned to the wall.

'Easy enough to stray,' he said. 'Or he might have had an accident. Horse problem. It's big country out there, brother.'

'Let's not forget McCall is from Texas. He'll be used to wide spaces.'

Brigham smiled. 'You think I'm worrying too much?'

'Nothing wrong with being concerned.'

'Joe and Lew are in town,' Brigham said. 'Might be a thought to set them free to go take a look.'

Joe Crown and Lew Riley were two of Brigham's top men. They had been with him from his first epic cattle drives across the mountains when he had brought in much-needed beef for the hungry miners in Hope. They had made the drive twice, through heavy snowfalls and dangerous country. Brigham knew them as dependable, trusty men who rode for the brand and never backed away from danger.

'Could work,' Seth agreed.

An hour later Crown and Riley rode out of Hope, carrying extra supplies and set their horses on the trail that would lead them to the area McCall would be expected to be in.

'If he's out there, boss, we'll find him,' Riley said.

Brigham watched them go from the boardwalk outside the jail. If anyone could find McCall it was Crown and Riley. He sensed Seth moving alongside, felt his brother's hand on his shoulder.

'Still playing mother hen,' he said. 'You always were the worrier.'

'Man like Jess McCall doesn't go missing so easily.'

Beyond Hope the high peaks were framed against the wide sky, only a few scattered clouds showing. The air was fresh and clean. It was beautiful country. There was a serenity to it that gave a man pause to count himself lucky living where he did. But there was another side to the coin. The mountain vastness held danger if a man didn't step carefully. The weather could change without warning. Storms could develop quickly. High winds and sudden rain. The terrain underfoot might catch a man off guard. Seth could understand his brother's caution.

'Let's hope Joe and Lew can find McCall.'

Seth saw Jacob, the third Tyler brother, crossing the street in their direction. Jacob wore a deputy badge now. Had for a couple of years now and had proved to be a dependable man at Seth's side.

Jacob had been the wild one of the brothers. When he had moved away from Hope he had got himself into trouble with the law through no fault of his own, with US Marshal Alvin LeRoy dogging him until the truth had emerged. At the time Jacob had a young woman helping him, Hannah Crane, and they had stayed together since. When Jacob had pinned on the badge, Hannah working in one of Hope's restaurants, he had settled down much to relief of his brothers.

'Any news on your missing Texan?' Jacob asked as he joined them.

Brigham shook his head. 'I just sent Joe and Lew to go look for him. If he's out there they'll find him.'

Jacob cuffed back his wide brimmed hat. He hooked his hands in his belt and surveyed Hope's busy main street. The town was much changed from the crude mining camp they had experienced when they had first ridden a few years back. Since that time the town had settled and grown, becoming firmly established. The tents and basic buildings had been replaced by permanent structures of timber and brick. Although the rush caused by the gold strikes had diminished, Hope had become a real community. There were ranches in the surrounding country. A couple of lumber mills. Freight companies and a stage line. There were a few mining businesses still in existence but the excesses of those early years had quieted down, leaving Hope to its quieter role.

'You going to wait around, Brig?' Jacob asked.

Brigham nodded. 'A while longer,' he said.

'Been a while since I got out to your place,' Jacob said. 'Seth here being a hard boss and all keeping me busy,' he added with a grin. 'How's the family?'

'They're fine.'

Brigham had two young children. Jessie his daughter was only a couple of years old. His son was four. Brigham and Judith, his wife, had named him Joel. It was in memory of the young man Joel Welcome, who had been with the Tyler brothers when they had first showed up in Hope. Joel had worked alongside them when they made their gold strike and though lacking in worldly experience had made up for it with an undiminished spirit. He had been killed by Red Karver. Karver had been one of the gang responsible for taking over gold claims by sheer violence. When Joel had stood up to them Karver had back shot him and set Brigham on the vengeance trail that ended with Karver dead and his gang eliminated. Even that had not been without tragedy. Judith had been kidnapped and her father William Thorpe killed. In the bloody conclusion to the affair Brigham had brought Judith back and they had later married and took over the ranch William Thorpe had established. The regular trail that led in and out of Hope had been named the Welcome Trail, in memory of the young man who had died.

'That's good to hear,' Jacob said. 'You give them my best when you see them.'

He took off at a slow stroll, nodding and speaking to people on the street.

'Few years back I would never have

imagined Jacob wearing a badge and making casual conversation with folk,' Brigham said.

Seth gave a quiet laugh. 'We were all rough around the edges the day we rode in here,' he pointed out. 'Now look at us.'

It was more than an hour later when Brigham was handed the telegram that had come over the wire from Marshal Teague in Culhane. He read the message, then passed it across to Seth.

'You know this town?'

'Only by name,' Seth told him. 'Nothing about Teague. But at least we know where Jess McCall is.'

'Seth, it looks as if he's in some kind of trouble.'

'Maybe I should take a ride over to Culhane and look into it. Deal with Teague lawman to lawman.'

'Something doesn't sit right here, Seth. Doesn't it make you wonder?'

'It does. While I'm gone you let McCall's people know what's happened. They might want to send somebody up to look into this as well.'

Seth Tyler's thought was correct. As soon as the message arrived in Beecher's Crossing and was handed to Henry Conway, Chet Ballard took it on himself to leave for Colorado.

He knew his partner. McCall was a competent man. Well able to look after himself, but even the most capable person could have a run of bad luck. When Ballard checked he learned the next available train wouldn't be leaving soon, so he was going to have to cool his heels until that time arrived, and hope McCall didn't get himself into too much of a bind.

6

They trailed quietly into town, coming in by the warehouses and cattle pens. If there were any signs showing the majority bore the Culhane name. Perry Culhane halted them outside the building that stated — *Culhane Freight Office*. A number of large, heavy wheeled wagons were drawn up nearby. In a pair of corrals the freight line's livestock moved around restlessly. Mules in one and powerful horses in the other. A number of Culhane employees were carrying out their daily tasks, glancing up as Culhane and his partners appeared.

'Just remember what we talked over,' Perry Culhane said as he dismounted. 'Stick with the story and we'll be in the clear.'

'The hell with all that right now,' Flag said. 'I need the damn doctor to pull this bullet out of me and do something for my face.'

He was hunched over in his saddle. The effects of his fall into the cook fire were showing now. Red flesh and swollen blisters. His shirt scorched and stained with blood from where McCall's shot had struck his right shoulder. A makeshift sling held his arm tight against his body.

'We'll get you there,' Perry snapped. He turned and signaled one of the nearby hands. 'Vern, see to the horses.'

'Yes, sir, Mister Culhane,' the man said and bunched the reins to lead the animals away.

The door to the freight office opened and Ira Begley appeared. He hurried to meet them.

'Good to see you back, Mister Culhane.' He looked Flag over. 'What happened to Flag's face?'

Meers said, 'Well it wasn't by catching too much sun, Begley.'

Begley ignored him, turned back to Perry Culhane.

'We got the feller,' he said.

'What *feller*?'

'Why him that stole Flag's horse and your gun. Marshal Teague done locked him up when I told him about stealing your things.'

'That sonofabitch is in town?' Flag said. He seemed suddenly nervous. 'Let me go and put a bullet in him.'

'Tell me what happened, Ira.'

'Yessir, Mister Culhane.' Begley was so full of his own importance he could barely speak coherently, but when Perry held up a warning hand he slowed down. ' . . . brought the deputy and we walked him to the jail. Teague said he would keep him there while he checked out this man's story. The marshal made me leave his office so I didn't get a chance to hear what the prisoner had to say.'

Perry caught the look in Meers' eye and gave a slight shake of his head. He understood Meers concern but this was a time to stay calm and not give anything away. As long as they backed each other and stayed with their story there was nothing to worry about.

'Funny thing was he made no fuss about it all,' Begley said. 'He was big enough to raise hell but he acted all peaceful. Hardly said a word.'

'We have to speak to the marshal ourselves,' Perry said. 'Put him straight on what happened out there. We need to get Flag over to the doc's first. This stranger burned him up, then put a bullet in his shoulder before he took off.'

'What did he do?' Begley asked.

'Looks clear he killed someone. Feller named Sturdevant. Set his body to burning. That was when we came on him and he set to trying to harm us.'

'But we beat him down and tied him up,' Meers said.

'Until the bastard got free and knocked me in the cook fire,' Flag said. 'An' then put a slug in me and took my horse.'

Begley looked suitably shocked. 'See,' he said. 'I knew he was a bad one minute I set eyes on him. So I went and brought Mort Pickett and we arrested him and took him to the jail. When we got him there he said nothing of much importance. Like he had nothing to worry about.'

Perry considered what Begley had told him. The one thing that puzzled him was the stranger's seeming acceptance of his situation. Riding calmly into town and letting himself be taken. The truth was the man had done nothing except try to help the victim. His actions when he had escaped would have been expected from anyone under threat. Yet he had, according to Begley, offered nothing in his defense. Maybe that was his way of covering himself.

'Has my father been told yet?'

Begley shook his head. 'I thought it best to wait.'

'You send one of the men out to the ranch. Let my father know there's a problem.'

Begley did that, dispatching one of the workers to ride out to Boxed-C.

'Buck, we'll take Ty over to the doc's.

Then we need to go see Marshal Teague. Get this thing cleared up. Right?'

Meers nodded. 'That's right,' he said.

* * *

A half-hour later Perry Culhane, with Meers slouching behind him, entered the jail. Marshal Teague was back behind his desk dealing with paperwork, and he looked up when Perry came in. The expression on his face warned Perry he had been expected and not to take anything for granted.

Teague squared up the documents in front of him. Leaned back and laid his hands flat on the desk, waiting.

'We come about this prisoner you got locked up,' Perry stated.

'I figured you would sooner or later. And by the way, his name is Jess McCall. Just so we don't get into any confusion over who we're talking about. He volunteered to stay in a cell while I check out his story, so technically he isn't a prisoner.'

'That pissant stole Perry's gun and Flag's horse,' Meers said loudly. 'Shot Ty to boot. What else do you damn well need to check?'

Perry cringed at the outburst. The last thing he needed was Buck Meers losing control.

'You have to excuse Buck,' he said. 'He's upset because his friend got hurt. In a way you can't blame him, Marshal.'

'Almost the same as I can't entirely blame McCall for getting a tad riled because somebody hit him, dragged him and generally gave him a hard time.'

Meers bristled.

'We found him standing over . . . '

Perry cut in sharply. 'Marshal, we came to tell you what happened. Not to throw accusations around before all the facts have been gathered. All I can tell you is we came across this McCall feller standing over a burning body. He attacked us and we defended ourselves.

We had him restrained but he broke free and ran. When we went after him he shot Ty Flag and escaped.'

Teague considered Perry's words. He leaned forward and pushed something across the desk. It was Perry's Colt.

'That yours?'

Perry managed a nervous smile. 'Why, Marshal, you know it's mine.'

'Just wondering why a guilty man would keep it and the horse you said he stole and ride into this very town with them both. McCall doesn't strike me as a foolish man. Sets a man to wondering. Wouldn't you think, *Mister* Culhane?'

Perry made a step forward but Teague picked up the Colt. 'Have to keep this as evidence for the time being. I'm sure you'll get it back once we sort all this out.'

'I'll get it back, Teague. You can be sure of that.'

Teague allowed himself a thin smile. 'Nice to be sure,' he said.

Perry picked up Meers' sharp intake of breath. He turned and stared at the man, his head moving slightly.

'Thanks for your time, *Marshal*. We have to go see if Flag is done at the docs. You need us we'll be around.'

Teague slid the Colt into a drawer. Made a point of locking it securely. 'If I want you don't worry. I'll find you.'

7

Jess McCall picked up some of the conversation Marshal Teague was having with Perry Culhane and the man called Meers. They were sticking to their story which left McCall out on a limb. It seemed Teague was unsure but Perry had two friends to back him and McCall *was* a stranger in the area. He heard the jail door close as Perry and Meers left. A few moments later Marshal Teague came into the cell area and stood facing McCall through the bars.

'I heard,' McCall said. 'They got their story together. There's three of them and I don't have anyone to back me.'

'Just listen first. I see it this way. You're new to this part of the country, right? Ever been this way before?'

'No.'

'Here to make a deal with a man over

to Hope. To buy breeding cattle?'

'Right.'

'So tell me, Mister McCall, why would you set a man on fire who most likely you didn't know? Tell me, McCall? Why would you do that?'

McCall spread his hands in gesture of having no idea.

'If that train hadn't come off the tracks I wouldn't have been in the area. Just my bad luck I decided to ride on to Hope instead of sitting it out. I really picked a bad day coming by this way. Now your Perry Culhane can tell it a dozen ways from breakfast but he's a damned liar.'

'I'm inclined to agree with you. But unless I can have him in here and admitting to what happened, McCall, it's his telling against yours. Hate to say it but the Culhanes throw one hell of a wide loop around the town. Right now he'll be out there spreading his side and passing out free drinks to anyone who'll listen.'

Teague showed the keys to the cells

and unlocked McCall's door.

'Step out and stretch your legs while we try and figure this mess out.'

'Just so you know, Teague. I'm not about to leave until I get this settled. Perry Culhane's accused me of murder. I can't let that stand. I won't. Better get used to it because this town ain't putting me down for something I didn't do.'

They walked back into the office where Teague poured them both fresh coffee.

'Perry Culhane is a rare piece of work. It's only because of his father he gets to throw his weight about. The Major is a hard man. Over the years he's protected Perry. Covered for every time he's done something wrong. Cost him money as well. The son is nothing like his father. He plays on the old man's influence. Uses his old man's name to get him whatever he takes a fancy to. You've got a taste of the town. If it wasn't for the Major, Culhane would lose half its businesses. Boxed-C has clout. Big enough to matter. The Major — well, he sees Perry as taking over when he can't run the ranch any longer.'

'There any other family?'

'The Major lost his wife years back. No other children. Just Perry.'

'Must be a disappointment to him,' McCall said.

Teague managed a sympathetic smile. 'Have to admit Perry hasn't grown up anything like his father.'

'But he *is* family.'

'There is that.'

'So should we expect a visit from the Major?'

'He'll be here once he gets news about what's happened.'

'He going to ride in with his crew backing him?'

'That's not the Major's way. He doesn't need a crowd of guns behind him. Only one who might come in with him is Cole Landers. Boxed-C foreman. Good man. Well respected. He's loyal to the Major. Landers and Perry don't get along.'

'Doesn't surprise me.'

'I need to ride out the way you came in,' Teague said. 'Take a look around.'

He stood and went to the gun rack. Took down a .44-40 Winchester. He loaded the rifle with shells from a box. Did the same with a handgun. He had just finished when the door opened and his deputy came in. Mort didn't conceal his surprise at seeing McCall.

'I'm riding out to take a look around, Mort,' Teague said. 'McCall, here, has agreed to stay here until we get this sorted.'

'He a prisoner?'

Teague put on his hat. 'Right now he's helping me with my inquiries,' he said. 'Mort, there's a difference of opinion over what happened. Until it's clear McCall is to be treated fair. Understand?'

Mort looked between the two men. 'I guess. It's kind of unusual, huh?'

'It is. While I'm gone, Mort, you're in charge. Take no nonsense from anyone. And I mean *anyone*. This is what you're paid for.'

'What about the Major?'

Teague picked up his gear and made for the door. He turned.

'Him too. Major Culhane doesn't own the law in Culhane, Mort. Remember that.'

When the door closed behind Teague the silence stretched. McCall topped up his coffee.

'You want me back in that cell?' he asked amiably.

'Might be for the best.'

McCall wondered for who.

Mort was looking nervous as he followed McCall and secured the cell door. He went back to the office and perched himself in Teague's chair. Mort wasn't too happy with the way things were going. He had a better understanding of the situation, knowing that the marshal was handling the matter in his own way and wouldn't make any rash decisions. Even so, he was feeling nervous at being left on his own. Mort had been Teague's deputy for almost two years. He had respect for the man. John Teague ran an honest office. He kept the streets of Culhane quiet and safe. Brooked no interference with the law and he was one of the few men in town who stood up to the Major. Mort admitted he was not exactly in Teague's league. He wished he had more to offer. With the marshal at his side he was able to handle most anything. Right now, on his own, with the man called McCall in one of the cells, and knowing the way things might go, Mort Pickett was unsettled.

He started when the door rattled and opened.

Ty Flag stood in the opening, his appearance causing Mort's unease to increase.

Flag's arm was in a sling. His burned face was marked by discolored flesh and blisters, his eyes wild with anger.

'I hear right that bastard is locked up?'

'Marshal has him here voluntarily,' Mort said.

'Has he now. Well that suits me just fine.'

Flag had his Colt pushed behind his belt, set so he could reach it with his left hand. He turned towards the cell block.

'You can't go in there,' Mort said, pushing the chair back as he stood.

'You damn well watch me,' Flag snapped. He yanked out the Colt as he spoke, dogging the hammer back. 'I got something to settle with that son of a bitch.'

The inflamed flesh of his face gleamed because of the ointment the doctor had applied in order to cool his burns. It added a further menace to his already angry appearance.

Mort reached for his shotgun leaning against the wall close by. He brought it into view, dogging back the hammers and leveling it on Flag.

'I mean it, Ty. You can't do this. The man hasn't been accused of any-thing . . . '

When Flag heard the double click of the hammers being cocked, he twisted around. He stared at the black muzzles of the scatter gun.

'What you goin' to do? Shoot *me*, Mort?'

Mort surprised himself by holding the shotgun steady even though he was scared.

'Don't push me into it, Ty. We all need to step back from doing anything stupid.'

Neither of them had seen or heard the man who had stepped into the open doorway. But they heard him when he spoke.

'The deputy is right, Flag. Put away your gun and leave. *Now.*'

It was Magnus Culhane.

The Major.

8

Ty Flag faced Culhane. Still angry. The Colt in his hand still high, the hammer back. He glanced across at Monk, then back to his employer. For a few seconds his anger held him undecided. Then he eased down the hammer and let the revolver sag in his hand.

'I understand your hurt, Flag, but this is not the way,' Culhane said. 'Let me deal with it. I want you to leave. *Now.*'

The commanding tone deflated Flag's mood and he stepped away, turning and walking out the jail.

'You can lower your weapon as well, Pickett,' Culhane said.

The Major closed the door. He was a striking figure, dressed in well-cut clothes, his cord breeches tucked smoothly into knee-high tan boots. Under a dark jacket his white shirt held a slight sheen. He carried his pearl-gray hat in his gloved hands. Culhane carried himself well, his back straight, a leftover from his military service, and his head was held high. Though in his early fifties Culhane could easily pass for a younger man. His dark hair and mustache showed no gray and his clear brown eyes showed a healthy shine. He presented himself as a man in full control.

'Deputy, may I speak with your *guest*?' The Major had a slight curl to his lips. 'I have been informed that he has not been charged with any crime.'

'No, sir, Major. Marshal Teague has agreed that he be detained here voluntarily while he investigates. He's in the cells. You go on through, Major.'

Culhane paused to hold his jacket wide. 'No weapons. You know I don't carry a gun.'

'No, sir.'

McCall heard the measured tread as Culhane crossed the office and faced him through the cell bars. They took a moment to size each other up before Culhane spoke.

'I've been hearing about you, Mister McCall.'

'Nothing good I'm certain.'

'Depends on which side you're on.'

'Of the bars you mean?'

Culhane managed a thin smile. 'I like a man with a sense of humor.'

'I prefer that to getting shot at.'

'Your visit to our territory has been something of a disappointment I take it?'

McCall pushed up off the bunk and crossed to face Culhane through the bars. He noted casually that the Major matched his height. A big man in more ways than one, he saw.

'Let's not dance around, Major. You've had your telling of the story. I've got mine. Something tells me we're bound to disagree. Your boys will tell you I killed some feller and set him on fire. I saw it different. Your boys decided to make an example of me and we tangled. Hell of a mess, Major. Look at it from my side. I barely been here long enough to catch my breath. Don't know a body to call friend. And I'm supposed to have murdered some feller I still don't have a notion about. Way I see it there ain't any good reason why I should.' McCall took a moment, watching for any reaction. 'So where do we go from here?'

'All I want is the truth.'

'At least we agree on that. Major, you want the truth? Go ask your boy. I can't say more than that.'

'I *will* find out,' Culhane said.

Culhane held McCall's steady gaze for a time, then turned about and walked away. McCall heard the jail door close behind him. He gripped the cold bars of the cell. Mort appeared.

'From what I heard things ain't changed much.'

'Mort, you catch on fast.'

'Hell, I'm not the sharpest feller ever but even I can see things ain't as cut-and-dried as Perry Culhane says.'

'Nice to hear you say that, son. Let's just hope your Marshal Teague can find out what really happened.'

'If there's anything to find he will.' Mort looked out the barred window of McCall's cell. 'It's going to be dark soon enough. Sure hope the boss gets back before then.'

McCall picked up on the nervous edge to Mort's words. The deputy was suddenly walking a thin line. As if he was expecting something to happen once darkness fell. He watched as Mort retreated to the office and stood gazing out through one of the windows.

That was all he needed. His lawman watcher getting an attack of nerves. McCall suddenly felt the cell close around him and he didn't like the feeling one little bit.

He knew one thing for certain.

If something was about to happen he needed to get out from behind the bars of his cell. Being trapped in the confined space of the cell left him powerless. If Perry decided McCall dead was a way out he might send in one of his paid guns to do the job. Jess McCall would stand up and face any man in an equal contest without hesitation. He didn't favor being cut down without a chance to defend himself.

He hoped that if it came down to it Mort would be able to defend the jail and its prisoner . . .

9

The Major maintained a working office in town. It was in the Culhane Real Estate building, that stood some way along the main street from the jail. From where he was seated behind his desk Magnus Culhane was able to watch the activity on the street. Right now, his gaze fixed on the law office, Culhane had a worried expression on his face. His brief visit with the Texan McCall, had left him with more questions than answers. Culhane didn't like being in the dark. He was hard but an honest man and believed he treated people fairly. He prided himself on being able to recognize a man's true worth from what he heard from that person's mouth — and Jess McCall didn't strike him as being untruthful, or deceitful.

The problem there then was if

McCall was telling the truth, someone else had to be lying. Perry, backed up by Flag and Meers, had presented him with their side of the story. Initially Culhane had taken his son's word, but after his talk with McCall an edge of doubt had begun to creep in. The man had offered a straight set of answers. There was no denying that.

There was a reluctance to accept Perry might be lying. The problem was Culhane's son had done it before. And the Major knew he had allowed it to happen. Covering for the boy was something he had come to accept. He was Perry's father and no matter how he looked on his son's behavior he felt obliged to protect him. It was, he understood, a requirement of being a parent. Only this time, if it came out that Perry *was* involved in an actual death, then even Culhane would have to step back and shoulder the responsibility.

He reached for the open bottle of whisky on his desk. The thick glass tumbler held traces of his earlier drink. Culhane topped up the glass. Raised it to his lips and drank. The whisky was a fine blend and went down smoothly. He normally enjoyed the sensation. Today was different. The liquor gave him little pleasure.

It came into Culhane's mind that despite the trappings of success surrounding him, the ranch and his other enterprises, his life had lost much of its purpose. Since the death of his beloved wife there had been an emptiness he could not fill. He had thrown himself into his business empire, devoting himself to making it his world. In that he had succeeded and his plans for increasing his wealth filled his days. Yet Magnus Culhane was missing the most important thing to make his existence complete.

Family. The lynchpin to hold everything together. In that respect Culhane admitted he had failed since his wife died.

Perry, his son, who should have been the one factor to make sense of all

Magnus Culhane worked for. The young man was selfish. He thought of no one but himself. He traded on his father's feelings. Used his influence to get what he wanted. Few of the Boxed-C crew had any respect for him. Though Perry was supposedly part of the work force he spent as little time as possible doing anything productive. The foreman, Cole Landers, had long ago realized Perry's disinterest in the day-to-day workings of the spread. He made sure he stayed away from Perry as often as he could. His respect for the Major made him hold his tongue. And Perry knew that too. Strutting around the ranch and making everyone under-stand who he was.

It was a relief to them all when Perry stayed away. Living in town and spend-ing his days at *The Golden Deuce* saloon, always accompanied by his two *friends*, Buck Meers and Ty Flag. The three of them hung around together. Drinking. Gambling. Pestering the women who worked in the town's saloons.

The working girls, who made their living by offering their favors to anyone who paid the going price, were reluctant to associate with the trio. Risk was part of their trade, but there were limits, and Perry and company could be relied on to go over those limits. Once they got a few drinks inside them the three became abusive. Sometimes violent. And more than one of the girls suffered at their hands on occasions. Perry himself had a vicious streak and he seemed to enjoy hurting the girls. They didn't like it but there was little they could do. Sex and violence together brought their own problems. If a girl was mistreated it was accepted as part of the business.

Perry Culhane always bought himself out of trouble. And if he was unable to manage his father would cover for him. Culhane influence and Culhane money carried a great deal of weight. That plus Culhane's lawyer, always there when needed, managed to keep Perry free from any real punishment.

The Major, while carrying the guilt for his son, always came through. In the aftermath Perry would be contrite, promising to stay out of trouble. Which he would do — until the next incident.

His father, aware he had to keep trying, would breath a sigh of relief when Perry decided to ride to town, Meers and Flag with him. They had a similar mark on them when it came to doing what they were paid for. As part of the spread's crew their actual work came to very little productively and Perry always covered for them. The Major had decided it was less of a problem if he turned a blind eye, telling himself they were at least companions for his wayward son. Not the men *he* would have chosen but Perry seemed to favor their company. It meant Perry was not on his own.

Culhane always made sure Perry had money in his pocket. That way he was hoping to ensure Perry had no need to find any other means to fund his reckless lifestyle. Secretly he was disappointed, almost shamed by the young man's wasted life. He knew his late wife would have wanted him to ensure their son was treated fairly. So he gave Perry the money, knowing he was not dealing with the matter correctly. He saw it as a way of buying himself some release from the guilt he carried. He wasn't buying happiness, simply putting off admitting his failure.

Culhane knew the people in town were dissatisfied with Perry's behavior. They accepted it under sufferance. The Culhane name was paramount. The Major was a big investor. He supported the town, surely owned much of it, and was more or less its keeper. It was another source of embarrassment to Culhane that Perry often used his father's name to get what he wanted in town. The sadness was in the fact the majority of townspeople sympathized with him. Understood how the younger man traded on his father's reputation. That understanding did little to cancel the resentment.

The day-to-day business of running

his ranch and the enterprises in town kept Magnus Culhane occupied. He immersed himself in it. Using the operations to fill his mind. Letting them blot out the problems with his errant son. At the back of his mind, always there, was the dread that one day Perry would go too far. The father could cover for the son, but only up to a point.

If Perry took one step too far his father's influence and money might not be able to rescue him. Culhane was starting to consider that day might be closer than he wanted to imagine.

He heard a knock on his door and called out. The door opened and Ira Begley stood there, hat in hand.

'What is it, Begley? Freight business can't wait? I have other things on my mind right now. Just don't need any of your piddling nonsense.'

Begley bobbed his head. Managed an ingratiating smile.

'I was passing on my way home, sir. Wondered if there was anything I could do.'

Begley balanced the books down at the freight office. Looked after the financial side of the business. Culhane couldn't fault the man's work. He just didn't like the man. His fawning attitude grated on Culhane's nerves. The manner in which he portrayed himself as somehow higher up the ladder than he really was.

'Thank you for your concern, Begley. I have everything under control. Now, if you will excuse me.'

★　★　★

Ira Begley made his way up the street, face still flushed with embarrassment. *Damn the man.* Dismissing him out of hand when he had been ready to help. First being sent packing from the jail, now Culhane. He felt slighted. Pushed aside when he held out the hand of . . . he saw the lights of *The Golden Deuce*. Shining against the coming dusk. He thought of his lonely room in the lodgings he used. Maybe a drink

— a couple of drinks — would help.

He pushed in through the batwing doors and took in the sights and sounds. Although it was not yet evening as such the place was half empty. Only the long bar held a number of customers. Begley crossed to the long bar and found himself an empty space. He asked for a beer and a whisky chaser. When they came he paid and picked up his drinks, found an empty table and sat down. Behind him a mechanical piano was banging out sound. If he stayed long enough he would hear the same tunes over and over. Right now he didn't mind. The noise helped him drown out the voices of rejection.

'*Hey, lookit who I found*. Damn me, it's Deputy Begley. The man who captured our big bad man.'

Begley looked up and saw Perry Culhane standing grinning at him. Buck Meers was just behind him and the scorched face of Ty Flag hovered close.

'Mind if we join you?' Perry said.

'No,' Begley said eagerly. He liked the attention.

The three pulled in chairs and crowded the table. They had a bottle with them. Perry topped up glasses.

'Hell of a day,' Meers said.

'You really think so?' Begley said, a sullen tone creeping into his voice.

Perry leaned forward. 'This a celebration, or a wake, Ira?'

'What am I supposed to think? Teague has that Texan sitting around the jail like he's an innocent man. Your father more or less just sent me packing when I offered my help. Be truthful, it's been a dogshit day.'

'Saw the lawdog riding out of town a while back,' Flag said. 'You think he's gone looking for the feller that Texan killed?'

Perry threw him a hard scowl. 'Damned if I know.'

Flag winced as a jolt of pain burned his shoulder. He downed the whisky in his tumbler.

'Way I see it we'd be doing this town

a favor if we took that *hombre* out of jail and strung him up. Right now he's sitting pretty back there. Probably laughing at us.'

He had already had a fair amount of whisky as he attempted to dull the pain of his shoulder. It wasn't working as it should. Simply making Flag more aggressive.

'*God-damn-it*,' he said loudly, rising out of his seat. 'I'm for going down there and busting that Texan out of his cell. Show him he can't make fools out of us. You boys seen what that yahoo done to me. I say we drag him out and give him a Culhane welcome.'

There was a ragged chorus of assenting voices from the bar.

'Ty, sit down and shut your damn mouth,' Perry said. 'You trying to work up a lynching party?'

'Wouldn't be a bad idea,' Meers said. 'Cure our problem with Sturdevant . . .'

He realized what he'd said the moment he spoke. Out the corner of his eye he saw Begley's wide-eyed stare and saw that the man was making a calculated guess.

Perry glanced in the direction of the bar. No one had heard. The men lined up there had only one thing on their minds — the next drink.

Perry tipped the whisky bottle and filled up Begley's glass again.

'Don't pay Meers no mind there, Ira. I guess we're all getting a little strung out here. Buck's just worried we might be forgetting we need to let the marshal handle this. Right, Buck?'

Meers swallowed his own drink. 'Yeah. I mean this is enough to shake any man's nerves. Seein' that burned feller and then taking on that rough-neck Texan an' all.'

Ira Begley downed his drink. He pushed his chair back and turned from the table.

'Going already?' Perry said.

'I'm not much of a drinker. You know that. Better I get some food down me.'

He walked out of the saloon without another word.

'Loose mouth is what you got,' Perry said to Meers. 'You said enough to make Begley start to think.'

'He'll have forgotten by the time he has his meal,' Meers insisted, though even he wasn't convinced.

'If he starts spreading the word,' Flag said. 'Jesus, Perry, the goddamn marshal is convinced that McCall feller didn't do it. He ain't even arrested him. This comes out we'll swing for it.'

Perry tossed down another whisky, his mind racing with possibilities. Trying to come up with something — anything that might give them a way out.

'Ease off, fellers. Teague is out of town. McCall is in the jail. Gives us a chance to make sure Begley don't decide to get talkative.'

'What you aiming to do?' Meers said. 'Gun him down in the street?'

'I'd do that if I thought I could get away with it. We find him and do it quiet like.'

'Wait 'til he comes out that eating

place he always uses,' Flag said. 'He never goes anywhere else.'

'We talking crazy or something,' Meers said. He lowered his voice. 'Murder is what we're thinking about.'

Perry leaned in closer. 'What we did out at Sturdevant's place was worse. You forgot that? We need to cover ourselves. So we got to make sure Begley doesn't say anything that might get people thinking.'

'Hell, we didn't set out to kill Sturdevant. Too much whisky and it got out of hand,' Meers mumbled under his breath, reaching for the bottle again. Before he could lift it Perry grasped his wrist. 'Leave me be,' Meers said, jerking his hand free.

The batwings swung open as a trio of men came in, crossing to the bar to loud hails from friends.

'Right now we got a chance to stop Begley getting people suspicious,' Perry said. 'Long as we play smart. Now Begley might speak up, or he might not. You've given him enough to go talk to

Teague when he gets back. If he does that's only going to make that lawdog think hard about what happened.'

'Me, I'd put a couple of slugs in the little pissant,' Flag said. 'Let me do it, Perry.'

'You and that damned gun,' Meers snapped. 'Always wanting to shoot someone.'

'You're not thinking clear, Ty,' Perry said. 'A body could identify you from a mile off. Face all burned. Arm in a sling. And guns attract attention.'

'Show up with your face like that you'd likely scare Begley to death,' Meers said.

'Best you stay here,' Perry said. 'Leave this to Buck and me.'

A few men were wandering away from the bar in the direction of the door and Perry nodded at Meers. They stood and fell in with the exiting men. They followed the others and wandered casually to the exit, easing themselves out through the door. Darkness had already dropped. Lamps had been lit behind windows. As the bunch of men dispersed Perry and Meers moved along the boardwalk. They were heading for the eating house where Begley would be taking his meal. As they walked by the window, unnoticed by the occupants they were able to see Ira Begley at one of the tables, bent over his food. They moved on by. At a store, owned by Major Culhane, Meers sat on one of the chairs lined up and watched the eating house while Perry went inside to buy tobacco. He spent some time with the proprietor, simply passing time until Meers caught his eye through the window, nodding to indicate Begley was on the move.

★   ★   ★

Ty Flag stared at the nearly empty bottle. His belligerent mood had worsened the longer he sat downing whisky. He was wallowing in self-pity, blaming the world for his problems — and concentrating on the tall Texan named McCall. The man was the reason Flag was in constant pain from his burned face and the hole in his shoulder. He refused to even acknowledge that he and his partners had created the situation that led to McCall hitting out at them. What mattered was that Flag had been hurt and made to look a damn fool.

He snatched up the bottle and poured whisky into his glass. It stung his burned, cracked lips when he drank. Flag banged the glass down on the table.

'Hey, Ty, you all right?' one of his friends called from the bar.

'Do I look all right?'

Flag pushed to his feet, swaying slightly. Even the effort of moving made his shoulder pulse with pain. He pulled his Colt from behind his belt.

'Go easy with that thing in here,' the bartender called.

He knew Flag of old. When the man drank too much he became aggressive. With the added pain of his injuries he was becoming increasingly angry.

'Go easy? I'll go easy when I settle with that Texan . . . ' Flag moved on heavy feet to the door. 'Any of you boys with me? Time we got 'er done.'

He shouldered his way through the batwings and across the boardwalk, almost stumbling when he went down the steps. He didn't even notice the men who followed him.

Flag weaved his way down the street. He could see the windows of the jail, light showing through the glass. He raised his Colt, hammer back, and triggered a shot that shattered glass.

★   ★   ★

Mort had sent out for food for himself and McCall. He picked up the tray holding a plate of stew and made his way through to the cells. He had the tray balanced in one hand as he unlocked McCall's door.

'Smells good,' McCall said.

'Always good from Casey Biggs' place,' Mort said.

He swung open the door to pass the tray over, McCall stepping forward to take it.

It was then that one of the jail windows was smashed, the crash of a shot sounding, the slug passing through the office to take a chunk of timber from the gun rack.

Mort's head jerked around. The tray slipped from his grasp and dropped to the floor. The deputy snatched at his holstered pistol and ran for the jail door.

'*Don't . . .* ' McCall yelled.

Mort ignored his warning. He yanked open the door and went through.

The moment he showed himself on the boardwalk another shot rang out and Mort was turned sideways on, the slug embedded in his leg. He staggered and went off the edge of the boardwalk, slamming face down on the street.

★ ★ ★

McCall had followed close on Mort's heels, snatching a rifle from the gun

103

rack as he passed it. A long-barreled Henry .44 caliber repeater. McCall turned the rifle over and checked the slide on the underside. It showed the weapon was fully loaded. McCall worked the lever, just to be sure, and saw a shiny cartridge being ejected. Plenty more in the magazine and one in the breech.

As he reached the open door and stepped through he heard the shot that put Mort down.

He saw the figure of Ty Flag, his gun up and leveled. Two men were close at his side.

More men were coming out of the saloon.

'*McCall* — that's the sonofabitch who burned me,' Flag yelled, and swung his weapon around. 'I want that bastard . . . '

★   ★   ★

Ira Begley was walking out of the eating house. As he emerged he saw Perry and Meers closing in on him. A sudden panic gripped him and Begley found he was rooted to the spot.

'Time to talk, Ira,' Perry said quietly, but the threat was strong in his voice.

They were suddenly standing on either side of him.

'No,' Begley said, because he understood now, and knew Perry wasn't going to let him escape.

Shots rang out down the street. Near the jail.

Perry glanced that way and even in the lamplight he recognized Ty Flag. His gun was out, his second shot sending Deputy Monk to the ground.

And seconds later the tall figure of Jess McCall appeared from the jail.

People were running out of the saloon. Spilling from the boardwalk. Customers were emerging from the eating house, pushing by, unmindful of them.

Begley saw his chance and tried to follow but he felt Meers' hand close around his arm.

No one paid any attention as Begley was pushed bodily into the alley beside the eating house. Meers and Perry crowding him.

'You figured it out,' Perry said as he and Meers stood close. 'You know.'

'I . . . was only guessing,' Begley stammered. 'When Buck said . . . '

'I knew he understood,' Perry said.

'I wont say anything, Perry, not about . . . '

'Well we can't afford to take that chance, you piece of horseshit,' Meers said. 'Never did trust you. Always too ready to tell tales.'

Meers' right hand moved up from his waist and Begley caught a glimpse of something gleaming dully in the weak light. A moment later he felt a hard blow in the region of his ribs. Meers jerked his hand. This time there was a soft, tearing sensation and a spear of blinding pain. Begley would have screamed but he felt Meers' big, work roughened hand clamp over his mouth, blocking off any sound. The pain increased as Meers jabbed and jabbed again, stabbing and ripping, and even in his confusion

Begley knew he had been knifed. His legs slipped from beneath him and he went down on the ground. Into the trash and the dirt. He drew his knees up to his chest, curling up against the terrible pain, his hands clutching at his torn body where blood was starting to pour from the wounds, while the night grew even darker around him. As the world began to shut down for him Ira Begley lost all interest and he was dead before the sound of more gunshots reached the alley.

10

McCall acted out of nothing less than instinct as he saw Flag's Colt lining up on him. The Henry, already tracking, held, then spat flame as McCall eased back on the trigger. The .44 slug slammed into Flag's shoulder, no more than an inch from his other wound. Flag let out a startled yell and fell back, his revolver discharging into the air.

From somewhere in the growing crowd of men filling the street Perry Culhane yelled out.

'That's him. McCall. The one who attacked us. We saw him burn some poor bastard. Now he's shot Ty Flag.'

The scene froze for seconds. In that hesitant space McCall heard Monk's hoarse voice from where lay on the ground.

'Get the hell away from here, McCall. Perry's after a lynch mob.'

McCall heard.

And also picked up the rising yells from the crowd.

It was, he decided, less about standing his ground and more about saving his skin.

He didn't debate the matter. McCall turned about and broke from the street, his long legs carrying him into the dark alley that ran alongside the jail. He never once looked back. But he heard a number of shots and the harsh sound they made as slugs thudded into the walls of the ally. He reached the end and swung hard left, careering without pause along the back lots of buildings, striding over refuse and sundry pieces of junk.

Hell, Mrs. McCall, your boy is in a heap of trouble this time.

He maintained a tight grip on the Henry, glad the Marshal of Culhane kept all his weapons fully loaded. He wasn't about to go on a killing spree but it was as certain as night followed day he was not going to make it easy for the ones chasing him.

He only paused once, when he saw dark figures crowding the alley behind him, and McCall laid down a trio of shots, placing them above head height, but close enough to force his pursuers to draw back.

As he reached the far end of the street McCall saw the dark bulk of the livery stable. He broke clear of the last building and ran across the open space. He went around the rear of the stable, stepping inside the big rear doors. Familiar smells reached him. The sounds of restless horses. He moved quickly down the length of open stalls. He had a hope that he might see his own horse there, and for the first time since he had ridden into Culhane, McCall's luck dealt him a choice card.

His black horse stood, muzzle down in a hay trough, still saddled and from what McCall saw nothing had yet been removed from the animal. He leaned the Henry against the side of the stall, removed the tie rope and took up the reins. The black resisted for a moment, then seemed to recognize McCall. It followed him without any fuss. McCall picked up the Henry, swung into the saddle and urged the horse back the length of the livery and out through the rear doors. As he emerged he caught a dark figure moving into view. The flash of a steel barrel on a rising gun.

'*Hey*,' the man yelled. 'He's down here . . . '

McCall slipped his right foot from the stirrup and kicked out. He felt his booted foot thud against the man's chest, the force knocking him off his feet. As the man went down McCall gigged the black with his heels and it took off in a dead run, away from the livery and out across the open land behind the town. McCall had no idea where he was going and at that moment he didn't care. He just wanted to make some distance between himself and the town of Culhane. The black, having been fed and rested, bunched its muscles and raced forward.

He picked up dim shouts behind him. Bent low in the saddle because he knew what was to follow. Shots were fired. A fair number. McCall's luck held as the dark beyond the town lights prevented accurate fire. The only thing he needed to know was whether there might be any pursuit. If that happened his luck might vanish. He didn't know the country but those who might follow would.

He pushed the thought to the back of his mind. McCall didn't have any choice. Staying around in Culhane right now was asking for more trouble. He needed a place he could sit things out while he worked on a plan of action.

And then what?

The most sensible thing he could do was find Marshal Teague. Explain what had happened and allow the lawman to step in and take control.

McCall reined the black in, bringing the horse a slow walk. He saw pale light flooding across the landscape from a risen moon. Turning in his saddle he scanned the way he had ridden. Watching. Listening. The night was silent. Not even a wind soughing through the trees and brush. He pulled the horse in close to a sheltering stand of trees. McCall dismounted. Reached for his canteen and took a drink, reminding himself to refresh his supply when he came across a source of fresh water. He unbuckled one of the pouches and drew out a cloth wrapped bundle. Inside was the backup handgun he always carried. Checking the revolver McCall loaded it, then dropped it into his empty holster. The feel of the heavy gun on his hip gave him a comfortable feeling.

He stood for a while, resting his hands on the saddle. The black lowered his head and plucked at the grass.

'Tell you, son, when we get back home I'm considering stayin' in Texas full time. I can get me into enough trouble there without I need to visit Colorado.'

The black raised its head, nickering softly in what McCall decided was agreement. He stroked the glossy neck. McCall debated his next move, not sure what to do straight off.

'Horse, right now I don't have much of an idea what to do, so I reckon we should get back to where it all started. Come morning we'll see if we can backtrack and find that spot.'

McCall took his time considering his next move. There was a hell of a lot of country around him. Most of it consisting of slopes and tracts of thick timber. If he had wanted he could have kept on climbing, taking to the high slopes of the surrounding mountains. It was the kind of country where a man could lose himself for a long time, but that wasn't what McCall wanted. His ultimate goal was to clear his name. To find out just what kind of a mess he had gotten himself in. Hiding out in the tall timber like some kind of hermit wasn't going to help him do that. Sooner or later he was going to have to come face to face with the reality of his situation. It didn't sit lightly. On the other hand

Jess McCall had never been the kind to back away from anything and especially when he knew *he'd* done no wrong.

Damned if I'm going to start quitting now.

He led the black into the sheltering darkness of a deep stand of timber and brush. McCall tied the horse to a low branch. He was about to collect his blanket roll from behind his saddle then recalled he had been about to use them in an attempt to put out the flames covering the burning man. He might have done that if Perry Culhane and his partners hadn't shown and braced him. In the event he had lost his blanket roll.

That had been something small compared to what the burning man had lost, so he quit worrying about that. Recalling the dying man brought to mind what Perry and his friends had said about an Indian girl. It intrigued McCall as he tried to figure out what it meant. Had she been with the man he had come across? He pieced together what he had overheard. It seemed she had run off and was gone somewhere that would take her away from Perry and company. Finding her might help, but McCall had no idea which way she had gone. Or how far. So for the moment all he could do was wait until he could locate the spot where he had seen the burning man.

McCall stood and stared at the place where his blanket roll had been, shaking his head in wonder at how a man's life could change in a matter of seconds — and in his case not for the better. He loosened the short coat still bunched behind his saddle and pulled it on, buttoning it against the growing chill. No blankets. He'd lost his hat. Maybe things would get better come morning. *Maybe*. McCall decided he wouldn't have bet his last dollar on that.

McCall found a spot close to a patch of brush and stomped down the mossy place to crush any rough patches so he could make himself as comfortable as possible before he stretched out. He pushed his hands deep into the pockets of his coat and figured this was going to be the best he could get right now. He pulled the collar up around his ears and hoped he could get to sleep before too long.

11

A new dawn. Light spread across the high peaks. The chill of night receded. Shadow pulled back, showing the spread of greenery that covered the high Colorado landscape.

Jess McCall woke after an uncomfortable night. He stamped around to ward off the chill that had invaded his aching body. He went to where the black stood. He heard it grumbling as he took a drink from his canteen.

'You and me both, son,' he said. 'Hot coffee and a big breakfast is what we both need.'

He checked the saddle, making sure it was secure before he mounted up. He eased the black out into the open and sat for a while as he worked out his position. Then he gigged the restless horse into motion and headed out.

* * *

Four riders, who had also spent the night on the mountain slopes, came in sight of each other at about the same time McCall started out.

Marshal John Teague from Culhane.

The others were Seth Tyler riding with Joe Crown and Lew Riley.

They had all spent the night on the forested slopes and having resumed their individual searches, they came within sight of each other in the first light of day.

Teague saw the badge pinned to Seth's coat and eased his horse close. He pulled back his own coat to reveal his own badge of office to show the newcomer. 'I'm John Teague. Culhane.'

'Seth Tyler. Marshal of Hope. This is Joe Crown. Lew Riley. They ride for my brother Brigham.'

Teague nodded. 'The man going to sell stock to Jess McCall out of Texas.'

Seth eased himself in the saddle. 'Appears we're all tied in together on this.'

'I left McCall in one of the cells back in Culhane while I rode out here to try and make some sense out of all this.' Teague caught the expression on Seth's face and added, 'McCall's not under arrest. We figured it might be in his best interest he stay secure until I got back.'

'Might be in all our interests if we heard everything you have to say.'

Teague gave chapter and verse, bringing Seth and company up to date on the situation.

'This Perry Culhane,' Joe Crown said. 'He under suspicion?'

'Let's say my interest in him is growing. You have to understand. Perry is a man who grew up in his father's shadow. He had all the advantages and the money. Used to getting his own way and figures he can get away with most things because his father always covers for him. Now I don't like that. Far as I'm concerned Perry gets the same treatment as everyone else. Right from the start I didn't see a lot a sense in McCall having any reason to do what Perry is suggesting.

Stranger to the territory. Only rode our way because his train broke down. I looked at it every which way but damned if I could figure why he would kill this man. Just didn't make sense.'

'But Perry Culhane?'

'Don't like pointing the finger but Perry is a vicious feller. Gets nasty if he don't get his own way.'

'Nasty enough to be the one behind this killing?' Riley said.

'More likely than McCall?' Seth said.

Teague nodded. 'The way he's acted in the past it wouldn't surprise me.'

'This is your bailiwick, Marshal Teague,' Seth said. 'We'll pitch in. You give the orders.'

'Grateful. First off it's John. I figure we need to find this burned man. Take it from there and see what we can pick up. Didn't have any luck yesterday. Got too dark before I made much headway.'

He suggested directions for Crown and Riley and once they had moved off, he and Seth picked up an alternative route.

'It's big country around here. Few definite trails so a man has to cut his own,' Teague said. 'I don't have to tell you that, Seth, coming from Hope and all.'

'Town's pretty much settled now but once a man gets up country it's still pretty untouched.'

'Was always going to ride over and take a look at Hope. Only life gets in the way.'

'You have much in the way of problems?'

'Major Culhane likes things to go his way. We have some trouble from rowdy cowhands. Weekends mostly. Can't say I have that much of a problem with Culhane himself. He knows how I stand. We've locked horns a time or two. I do my job. Offer no favors if something comes from his men. They get treated the same as anyone. It's the way I work. Culhane sees that and gives me space.'

'Might be different if it turns out his son committed a crime.'

'I already been thinking about that,' Teague said. 'Face it if it comes.'

* * *

A couple of hours passed with no results. They rode steadily, searching for any tracks that might give them help.

'Something on your mind?' Seth asked. He had noticed Teague's increasing interest in the area they were riding through.

'I recall hearing about a man named Carl Sturdevant who had a place up here somewhere. If I recall he had a woman with him. Ute Indian. Was said he had a cabin around here. Just him and his woman. Never seen either of them. I mean they never came into town.'

'So he could be the one who got burned?'

'I can't see there being two Sturdevants in the area.'

Teague drew rein, took off his hat to run a sleeve across his brow. Seth had also noticed the heat had risen as the morning progressed. He could feel it on his back.

They sat their horses, scanning the landscape until Teague spoke up again.

'There,' Teague said, pointing ahead. 'Damned if I don't see a cabin.'

Seth followed his finger and picked out the shape of a structure through the trees and brush. They spurred their horses forward, breaking through the stand of timber and emerged on a semi-cleared area with a solid-looking cabin and small corral. A stream ran across the cleared section, providing a source of water. The cabin's door stood open. There was no movement to be seen.

Seth slid his rifle from its sheath and held it ready. Beside him Teague drew his own weapon. They let their horses close in on the cabin. Movement from the corral came from three horses penned there. As they got closer they saw a couple of chickens wandering loose, pecking at the ground.

From the cabin the view was impressive. The landscape fell away, fold after fold of timbered and green country. In the far distance higher peaks showed against the clean sweep of the sky. Seth knew the scenery well enough. It was part of what had drawn the Tyler brothers to Colorado themselves. A big piece of country with enough to satisfy a man. It had taken a while before they achieved what they wanted and some fighting to hold onto it. But they had persevered and were making a good life for themselves.

They stepped down from their horses, looped the reins around the corral post and went towards the cabin door.

'You getting a feeling things ain't right here?' Teague said.

Seth only nodded.

Close to the cabin they found a discarded Henry rifle on the ground. And there were sides of deer meat cast aside as well that someone had dropped in a rush, though the meat was swarming with flies now.

They stopped at the open doorway, taking in the wreckage of the interior. Every item of furniture had been smashed and cast aside. Crockery and cooking tools scattered across the floor. Food supplies dumped on the floor and trodden underfoot. Seth made his way through to the door leading to the far room, the door hanging from one twisted hinge. The scene was the same. The room wrecked. Clothing scattered across the floor.

'Seth, there's blood here.'

It was Teague who spotted the faint trail of blood spots that went out through the door.

'Looks like we missed those.'

'Easy when you're looking to find someone alive.'

They backtracked and saw the faint line of blood spots moving away from the cabin in the opposite direction they had been moving when they rode in. Now they could see them and also the scuffled prints that showed where someone had run. Not from calm, measured steps, but wide spaced from someone moving fast.

And something else.

A patch of scorched grass. Blackened and shriveled where a blaze had started. Then an erratic line moving away from the cabin, into and through the trees beyond the cleared area. More burn marks on the trees. And to one side of the scorched patch lay a gallon-sized metal can, with the unmistakable smell of coal-oil coming from it.

'Jesus,' Teague whispered.

Seth saw where he was looking. On a tree trunk the obvious mark left by a bloody handprint, fingers splayed apart. And more burn marks in the bark. They followed on, reluctant because they knew what they were going to find and there was no way they could back off now. They saw the deeper marks left by horses. Again leading into the trees.

A slope led them out of the timber to an open patch.

A clearing that showed more boot

prints. Hoofprints of a single horse coming in from a different direction.

And the charred and blackened form of a body, twisted and drawn in on itself, hands showing as gnarled claws. Eyes open but seared by the heat. The mouth frozen in what might have been a tortured scream. Lips shriveled back. Teeth in shrunken gums. Flesh split.

Teague sucked in a breath as he viewed the grisly image.

'McCall told it right. His burning man.'

Seth silently surveyed the corpse. Saw the charred grass around the body. Backing off he noticed the cast aside blankets some feet away. He pointed them out to Teague.

'McCall told me was going to use his blankets to try and put out the fire. That was when Perry and his two friends showed up.'

'We've got his far,' Seth said. 'Just one more question to answer. Where's this woman?'

12

Her Ute name translated as Mountain Spirit and she was of the Weminuche. She was of twenty-two summers. Hair so black it shone and her gray eyes were wide and looked on the world with undiminished interest. When she moved it was on moccasin-clad feet as light as a breeze, her lithe body smooth and supple beneath the soft buckskin dress . . . and her world had been full of promise as long as she was with her man . . . Carl Sturdevant . . . safe and secure in the cabin they had built together on the mountain slope. They lived their life in contentment . . . part of the land as it should be: She patiently taught him the ways of her people . . . schooled him how to live from the land and he gave her his language so they could converse . . . he taught her how to read . . . she spoke to him of the history of the Ute people . . . and life was good . . . he had come to their land as a hunter, alone, trusting, and the Utes had seen the peace in his heart . . . they had taken him in, letting him stay with them . . . teaching him their ways. He had learned, respecting the way they lived, only taking from the land what they needed and putting back what they were able . . . in his way he had given back much to them . . . satisfied to be with them . . . understanding their love of the wild Colorado mountains and what it had to offer . . . and when he had put his gaze on Mountain Spirit he had showed he wanted her . . . following what custom decreed until their courting time was over and she stayed by his side. When the tribe decided to move Mountain Spirit chose to stay with him and they travelled to the place where he would build their new home . . .

Life was good . . . they were happy in the cabin . . . until the three men had shown up. They had come by the cabin more than once and each time they came the distrust grew in Mountain Spirit because she saw in them evil, which her man could not. His trusting ways betrayed him. Often when they came she could smell the whisky on them. The more they came the stronger became her mistrust of them. And there was the way the three looked at her. Watched her as she moved about, their hungry eyes following her . . . they would stare at her and exchange glances, sly smiles on their faces . . . and Mountain Spirit was sure they meant harm to her and Sturdevant.

Of them all it was the man called Perry who disturbed her most. Mountain Spirit sensed the evil in him. His manner unnerved her, yet Sturdevant could not see the covetous way he feasted his eyes on her every move. She attempted to push the thoughts from her mind, not wanting to disturb Sturdevant.

But the day came when he was out hunting and she was alone in the cabin. He had gone looking for fresh meat.

Mountain Spirit had her own work. Sturdevant had been gone for a couple of hours when she heard the sound of horses. She went to the open door of the cabin and froze when she recognized the three riders.

Perry Culhane — Buck Meers — Ty Flag.

She knew they meant her harm. It took one look at their sweating faces. The whisky jug they were passing between them as they reined in and slid from the saddles, Perry stumbling towards her, a leering grin on his face as he fumbled with the buttons on his pants.

'This has been a time coming,' he rasped. 'And I waited too long.'

'No more waitin', bitch,' Meers said.

Mountain Spirit understood only too well what they intended. Despite the fear she felt she stood her ground.

'Hey, save a piece for me,' Flag yelled.

And Mountain Spirit's world erupted in a blinding flash of violence and terror as Perry lunged forward, hands reaching for her. She pulled back, one hand sweeping across his face, delivering a sound slap that rocked his head back. He retaliated by punching her across the jaw. She stumbled back inside the cabin, dazed from the blow and tasting blood in her mouth. Perry caught hold of her dress, jerking her off her feet, throwing her across the room. She slammed into the table and sprawled across it. The table toppled, throwing her to the floor, Perry following, his harsh laughter filling her ears with its ugly sound. He pounded and kicked her, dragged her upright and drunkenly struck her over and over until she was a bloody wreck.

Meers had followed and he began to drunkenly smash up the room, destroying anything he could get his hands on. She could hear things splintering and shattering as she struggled to her knees and crawled away from Perry's advancing figure. Felt his booted feet thudding against her body. Somehow she staggered upright, body burning with pain, and tried to escape his attack. He reached her at the door to the back room, flinging her bodily across the bed and fell across her, the stench of his alcohol breath in her face as he clawed and tore at her buckskin dress, baring her brown flesh. His hands were rough and clumsy as he pawed her body. His weight pressed her down on the bed as she fought him silently. She struck out at him, her small fists making little impression on him. She felt his fingers jerking at the hem of her dress, dragging it up her naked thighs . . . his rough hand reaching for her . . .

'Hey . . . get out here . . . '

It was Flag, his voice coming from outside the cabin.

The cry alerted Perry and he suddenly bunched a fist and struck Mountain Spirit across the side of her jaw. The blow snapped her head to one side and she dropped motionless, not even aware his weight had gone from her body.

* * *

As Perry lurched across the cabin, kicking aside broken possessions, he fell in behind Meers. They came out and saw Ty Flag holding his rifle on Carl Sturdevant. Sturdevant's own rifle lay on the ground alongside the fresh meat he had just returned with.

'Where is she?' Sturdevant yelled, his face dark with rage.

'Inside,' Meers said, grinning. 'Where a damn squaw should be. In the bedroom.'

'On her back,' Perry taunted. 'An' waiting for me to brand her. Son of a bitch you interrupted me . . .'

'Yeah, things were just starting to get hot,' Meers taunted.

'That's why he likes his Injun bitch,' Flag said. 'Likes 'em hot.'

Sturdevant gave a wild scream and launched himself at Flag. His move caught Flag by surprise despite holding a rifle. He slammed against him, pushing Flag back. Meers rushed in and clouted Sturdevant across the back of his neck with the barrel of his handgun. Sturdevant slumped to his knees, gasping in pain. Flag caught his balance and kicked out, his boot slamming across the side of Sturdevant's face. Blood burst from Sturdevant's torn lips. He was on his knees, head down, blood dripping from his slack mouth.

'Not so hot now, Injun lover,' Meers said.

'That what you want, squaw man? Your hot woman. I'll give you hot.'

Perry had spotted the gallon can holding coal oil standing on a stump beside the cabin door with a lamp waiting to be filled. He snatched it up, unscrewed the cap and stood over Sturdevant's slumped body. He was laughing recklessly as he tilted the can and began to douse Sturdevant with the contents, the air reeking from the fumes. Perry pushed the dazed man on his side and continued pouring until Sturdevant was drenched in oil. He pawed ineffectually as the oil splashed his eyes, coughing when he breathed in the fumes. Perry cast the empty can aside.

'No woman, mister, but you can have your hot time,' Perry chuckled.

He pulled a couple of Lucifers from his vest pocket, struck them against the butt of his holstered Colt, held up the matches as they flared. He cast the matches into the haze of fumes rising from Sturdevant's soaked clothing. There was a soft pop of sound as the fumes ignited, the flame spreading swiftly and engulfing Sturdevant in a halo of burning oil.

He twisted in growing agony as the oil burned at his flesh and clothing. Gained his feet and ran in blind panic, reason lost in the hellish grip of the fire. Heedless of direction he ran. Across the open ground and into the trees, slamming blindly into the trunks as he desperately tried to escape the searing heat.

'Yeehaw,' Perry yelled, 'never did know that boy could move so damn fast.'

With Meers and Flag on his heels Perry hauled himself into the saddle and the three spurred their horses in pursuit of the burning man . . .

* * *

Mountain Spirit, bloody and battered, vaguely aware that something terrible was taking place outside, had stumbled to the cabin door in time to witness what happened to Sturdevant. The sight was almost too much to bear, but she remained in the shadow just inside the opening as she watched her man run in sheer panic, flames trailing behind him as he crossed the open ground and vanished into the trees. She saw Perry and his partners mount their horses and follow.

She stared in stunned silence for what seemed an eternity before a sane thought entered her mind.

If she remained where she was the three would come back. Sturdevant would not. She had to get away. To make some distance from this place which was now lost to her forever.

There would be a time to grieve but it was not now. However she felt, if she was to stay alive, then she had to abandon this place.

She slipped away from the cabin, moving quickly in the opposite direction so she was hoping to avoid Perry Culhane and his friends. If they found her they would kill her because she knew what they had done.

So Mountain Spirit ran for her life.

She summoned up every ounce of strength in her young body, knowing that if they came for her their horses would cover ground much faster.

In her need to escape she became careless, stumbling and falling, ignoring the hurt to her body and thinking of only one thing.

Escape.

There was no thought in her mind of any destination while she ran. If she had even that would have been a hard decision. Her own people, her tribe, were many days distant, far to the north. The closest town was Culhane.

The place where Perry came from and going there held little appeal to Mountain Spirit.

In her blind rush she didn't realize she had retraced her steps a number of times and went no further than a mile from the cabin. Falling, turning around, slipping down slopes and banks, her already injured body receiving more damage, Mountain Spirit took her final steps and crashed through a thick growth of brush and stepped into empty air. She fell many feet, cushioned by the soft undergrowth and finally came to a jolting stop. Too hurt and weak to stand again she fell into an unconscious state and lay still.

* * *

It was there that Joe Crown and Lew Riley found her. The Tyler hands, searching the area, had passed her twice before Riley caught a brief glimpse of something deep in the brush at the base of a slope. Taking their heavy bladed knives they cut through the mass of brush until they were able to stand over the limp form of the young woman they would come to know as Mountain Spirit.

'What do you think?' Riley said. 'She alive or what?'

Joe Crown dropped to his knees and bent over the girl. Dried blood caked her face and exposed arms and legs. Apart from bruising there were numerous gashes and scratches from contact with thorny brush. Riley watched in silence as Crown checked the motionless form.

'Well?' he asked, unable to contain his impatience.

Crown stood, hat in hand as he scrubbed a hand through his hair.

'Go get blankets, Lew. We need to get this girl somewhere she can be looked at.'

While Riley returned to their horses Crown stood over the girl. Apart from the blood and the bruises and all, Mountain Spirit's tattered dress was wet from the exposure to the changing temperature. He had no idea how long she had lain where she was but it had to have been at least once overnight.

'Lord, girl, you've been through it.'

When Riley returned they gently lifted her slim form and covered her, drawing the blankets around her. They maneuvered out from the brush and carried her to their waiting horses. Crown climbed into the saddle and Riley passed up the limp form, holding her secure. They turned about and began the ride back to where John Teague and Seth Tyler were still checking the area round the body of Carl Sturdevant.

A fire was built some distance from where the body lay and water set to boil for coffee. Extra blankets were used to make the Indian girl as comfortable as possible.

'You think she'll pull through?' Riley asked.

'Fact she's still alive now tells me she's no quitter,' Teague said.

'We need to get her back to town,' Seth said. 'Let your doctor look after her.'

'Sounds a good idea to me,' someone said.

When they turned Jess McCall was walking into their camp, leading his horse by its rein.

13

McCall wasn't looking his best. Unshaven. Wearing travel-stained, bloody and tattered clothing but wearing a holstered Colt that looked in the right place on his hip. After introductions had been made and McCall took a mug of scalding coffee, he told Teague what had happened in Culhane.

'Bad as it might sound,' Teague said, 'I wouldn't have been bothered if you'd put Flag down permanent.'

'Things were a tad dicey,' McCall said. 'Way things were going somebody was ready to stir up a lynch mob, so I took Mort's advice and lit a shuck out of there.'

'How bad hurt is he?' Teague asked.

'Took a slug in the leg. Still had enough in him to tell me to get the hell out while I was able. Teague, you have a good feller there.'

'I'm sure he'll let me know that.'

McCall stood over Mountain Spirit.

'Hell, she don't look more than a kid,' he said. 'All in all that Perry Culhane and his boys have surely stirred up a hell of a mess.'

'You got my vote on that,' Crown said.

'I hope when this is all over,' McCall said, 'your boss still has some halfway decent cows to sell me.'

'Brig won't deal you anything but the best,' Crown said.

'He runs a fine outfit,' Seth put in. 'Brother or not I'd say one of the best in Colorado.'

They rested a while, then organized their return to Culhane. With more blankets wrapped around her Mountain Spirit was held in Crown's arm for the ride. He wouldn't even consider anyone else handling the young woman.

Teague and Seth took the lead, Crown and McCall behind, with Lew Riley riding drag.

'Be dark by the time we reach town,' Teague said.

'We should make a quiet entrance and take the girl straight to the doctor,' Seth suggested.

'That was my intention.'

'So what happened back there?'

'I'd figure Perry and his partners rode in and pushed themselves on the girl. Sturdevant showed up and tried to stop them. It went bad for him. When it happened the girl managed to break away. McCall rode in, tried to help Sturdevant and got overpowered.'

'He witnessed Sturdevant's death so they had to silence him. But he got away and that left them with a dead man and a missing girl. They were banking on her being too hurt and too scared to turn up in Culhane.'

'McCall showing up in town must have scared them. So they tried to turn everything around to put the blame on him.'

'You weren't convinced?' Seth asked.

'I wouldn't like to brace McCall. He looks more than capable, but he made a pretty convincing argument. I couldn't see any reason why a complete stranger would ride in and kill Sturdevant. McCall was only in the area because his train was delayed and he decided to finish his trip by horse.'

'But this Perry Culhane is a likely candidate?'

'Arrogant. Takes advantage of his father's position. Likes to take what he wants and push people around. Believes he's untouchable.'

'If he finds out the girl is alive . . . ' Seth said.

'Which is why we need to get her safely into town. Protect her. See what Perry does when he learns she's there.'

★   ★   ★

A chill wind was spiraling along Culhane's main street as they rode in. Joe Crown followed Marshal Teague to the doctor's office. Between them they carried Mountain Spirit inside. Lew Riley volunteered to take the horses to the livery and get them settled and McCall and Seth Tyler took themselves to the jail. There was a lamp showing, throwing light across the boardwalk. When McCall opened the door he saw Mort Pickett in a chair by the desk, his bandaged leg propped up on a three-legged stool. There was a wooden crutch leaning against the desk and a shotgun next to it.

'McCall, you're the last man I expected to walk through that door,' the deputy said.

'How's the leg, Mort?'

'It hurts. No thanks to that sonofabitch Flag.'

'Where is he?'

'*Flag?* Him and his two buddies are holed up in *The Golden Deuce*. They got a bunch of Boxed-C riders in there with them.' Mort leaned forward as he caught a glimpse of the badge Seth was wearing. 'Do I know you?'

'Seth Tyler. Marshal from Hope. Rode across looking for McCall here when he went missing.'

'Well you found him. You find Teague out there?'

'He's back,' McCall said. 'Down at the doc's.'

'He hurt?'

'Not Teague. Somebody else who likely can answer some questions.'

'About your burning man?'

'Yeah. We found him as well. Pretty sure he's this feller Sturdevant.'

Mort shook his head. 'Damn, McCall, this is one hell of a puzzle.'

'You had any telegrams come in while I been away?' McCall asked.

He crossed to the stove and filled three mugs, handing them out.

'Some feller name of Ballard. Said to tell you he's on his way from Texas.'

McCall's worn features creased into a grin. 'My partner. He doesn't like me going out on my own. Got this idea I'll get myself into trouble.'

'Sounds a smart feller,' Seth said.

'Next train in is 8.30 tomorrow morning,' Mort offered.

The door opened and Marshal Teague stepped inside. He crossed the office and looked Mort over.

'How you doing?'

'Doc Cavanaugh said I'll be fine in a couple weeks.'

'I go away for a couple days,' Teague said, a grin forming on his face.'

'How is the lady doing?' McCall asked.

Teague poured himself coffee. 'Doc says she'll come through. She'd been roughed about some. Cracked ribs. Fractured arm. Hit in the face and body. Plus the fact she must have knocked herself around some when she ran from that cabin and fell quite a piece. Suffered from exposure laying out there overnight, but Doc says she'll be okay with rest and food. His wife cleaned her up and put her into warm clothing. Now all she needs is time to recover.'

'She said anything at all?' McCall asked.

'Not a word yet.'

'Until she does we're no better off knowing what really happened.'

Seth glanced at the Texan. 'We have

your word Perry Culhane and his partners were there.'

'Only my word I saw them.'

'Good enough. And you've proven to me you weren't involved in Sturdevant's killing.'

'*Killing* — hell, I need to tell you something, Marshal, we had ourselves a killing while you were away,' Mort said by way of a subject change. 'An out-and-out murder.'

'Who?' Teague asked.

'Ira Begley. His body was found in the ally next to the eating house he always used. Must have happened around the time we had that fracas with Flag. Seems somebody knifed him to death. Pretty well butchered him from what I been told.'

'He that same feller who was playing deputy?' McCall asked.

'Yeah,' Mort said. 'Worked for Major Culhane. Office clerk and nosy parker.'

'Begley was a snooper,' Teague said. 'Worse gossip than any woman.'

'Maybe he learned something he

151

shouldn't have,' Seth said.

'Hard way to pay,' Mort said.

'You mind if I go find a room?' McCall said. 'Need a bath and a change of clothes. Then I'm going to get me a few hours' sleep.'

'I'll walk with you,' Seth said. 'I need to send a telegram to my brother Brigham. Let him know how things are.'

*   *   *

By the time McCall returned to the jail later he looked a different man. A visit to a local bath house, followed by a set of fresh clothing had tidied the outer man. He only stayed long enough to see if anything had happened before he left again. He made a further visit to the local doctor to inquire about Mountain Spirit and have his physical wounds tended to. He found Joe Crown still there, sitting beside the girl's bed. He refused to leave her side. Even his partner Lew Riley couldn't budge him.

'Never seen this side of him,' Riley said. 'Like he found a long-lost relative.'

Marian Cavanaugh, the doctor's wife, who was taking them upstairs to the room where Mountain Spirit lay, said, 'He seems extremely attached to her. You say you only met her a short time ago?'

'Yes, ma'am. It was Joe and me found her in the brush. Truth be told we thought she was dead but Joe wouldn't have it. Looked her over and said he could feel her heart still beating. Carried her all the way back to town on his horse. Wouldn't let no one else handle her. That's Joe. Once he sets his mind to something there's no changing him.'

The room was at the front of the house. It overlooked the street. Joe Crown was sitting on a cane seat, his gaze centered on the slight form of the Indian girl. She was covered by blankets with her arms exposed. One was covered by a bandaged splint. Her face showed the marks of the beating she had received.

'Didn't realize how much she'd taken,' Riley said.

'She'll recover,' Marian said quietly. 'We'll see she does.'

Crown raised his head, the first time he had moved since they entered the room. 'I ain't leavin' her, Lew,' he said. 'I want to be here when she wakes up.'

Riley said, 'No worries there, partner. Hey, you want me to sit a while? That allowed, ma'am?'

'I don't see any reason why not.'

'See you boys later,' McCall said and followed Marian out of the room.

As they made their way back down the stairs she touched his arm.

'You look as if you could do with some sleep yourself, Mister McCall.'

'You're right, ma'am. It's been a busy couple of days.'

He walked out of the office and headed along the boardwalk, searching for the hotel Teague had described to him.

He found it and went inside, asked for and got a room, where he shucked his boots, tucked his Colt under the pillow and climbed into bed.

He failed to notice, as he walked to the hotel, the man who paused when he caught a glimpse of the Texan. The man stared after the tall figure, then moved on, making his way to *The Golden Deuce*.

14

The man who had spotted McCall went directly to the table occupied by Perry Culhane, Buck Meers and Ty Flag. There were at least a half dozen other Boxed-C hands in the saloon. There were plenty of whisky bottles on show as well. A heavy pall of tobacco smoke drifted overhead.

The cowboy, one of Perry's close group, crossed immediately to speak with him.

'He's back,' the man said.

Perry raised his weary eyes. He had been drinking steadily for hours and he almost failed to catch what the man was telling him.

'*Who?*'

'That Texan. The big *hombre* who shot Ty before he lit out of town.'

Buck Meers responded faster. He paced himself when drinking and was many glasses behind his employer.

'*McCall?* You sure?'

'I'm sure. Hard to miss that damned big feller. Saw him going into the hotel.'

Perry slowly absorbed the information, reaching for the half-full bottle in front of him. He only managed to knock the bottle over. It would have spilled its contents across the table if Meers hadn't grabbed it.

'Not the time, Perry,' he said. 'We need clear heads here.'

'I ain't drunk,' Perry said, his words slurred.

'You're makin' a pretty good impression then.' Meers turned to the man who had just brought the information about McCall. 'Go take another look around town. If McCall's back it might mean Teague is. Take a couple of the boys. If you get a chance check the jail. Jake, keep this quiet. We need to know what we're dealing with here.'

With that done Meers called one of the Boxed-C men over and between them they pulled Perry to his feet.

There were a half-dozen small rooms on the upper floor. Meers decided the best thing for Perry was to lie down and sleep off the effects of the liquor.

'What do you want me to do?' Flag asked.

With his shoulder still heavily bandaged and held against his chest by a restricting sling he was still in some considerable pain and it took away any effective actions he might make.

'Wait until the boys come back from checking things out. I'm starting to get a bad feeling about all this, so we need to stay on top of it.'

★   ★   ★

With two other of Perry's crew following, Jake left the saloon. He got them to take a side of the street each and they started a thorough check. Thought it was approaching mid-evening there were still a number of people around. There were still stores open too.

Jake himself took a slow walk towards the jail and when he reached it he approached from the side, waiting until that part of the street was clear. He pressed to the wall and took off his hat, leaning forward to glance in the window.

Teague was there. So was the deputy, Mort, leg propped up on a stool. And there was a third man.

He was tall and solid, but the thing that took Jake's interest was the badge pinned to his shirt.

Another lawman.

Jake couldn't see the badge clearly enough to read what it represented.

For all he knew it could be a US Marshal badge.

Jake eased away from the jail, turned about and made his way back to *The Golden Deuce*.

If the man was a US Marshal matters were taking a different turn.

Jake was almost at the saloon when one of the other Boxed-C men reached him.

'You get anything?' Jake asked.

'I had words with Ostermann over at the gun shop. Across from the doc's. Seems he saw some activity there. Teague and a couple of newcomers. One feller took their horses off. The other stranger was carrying what looked like a young woman wrapped in a blanket. They took her inside. Too far away for Ostermann to get a clear look, but when one of the girl's arms showed he's sure it looked brown like an Injun.'

Jake said, 'Go find Fitch. Keep checking and see if anyone else saw anything.'

Flag was sitting on his own when Jake went into the saloon.

'Anything?'

'New lawman in Teague's office,' Jake told him. 'He might be a US Marshal, but I couldn't see his badge clear enough. He's in there talking to Teague.'

'That's all we damnwell need. You get anything else?'

'Sam had a word with Ostermann.

He saw Teague and a stranger carrying a woman into the doc's office. He couldn't be sure but he reckons she could be an Indian.'

Flag's face visibly paled. He snatched up his glass and downed the shot of whisky.

'That mean anything?' Jake asked.

'Mebbe so, mebbe not,' Flag said. 'You and the boys keep asking questions. I got to go check on Perry.'

Flag stood and clenched his teeth against a wave of pain from his ravaged shoulder. He pushed back the wave of nausea as he crossed the saloon, suddenly aware of the strong smell of tobacco smoke and the noisy atmosphere.

Son of a bitch, he thought. *The damned squaw.*

If she was able to speak then he and Meers and Perry could be in more trouble than they had figured. It had been a damn fool thing not chasing after that girl. But they had been too busy dealing with the Texan who had walked in on Sturdevant and spotted them. It had all started to get out of control after that. When the man, McCall, had escaped and they had gone looking for him thoughts about Mountain Spirit had slipped away. Perry had been too busy covering their tracks — and even that hadn't exactly gone as it should.

Making his way upstairs Flag went to the room where he had seen Perry go in. The door opened and Buck Meers stepped out. Flag told him what Jake had found out.

'Don't let Perry know yet. State he's in he'll go hog wild and do something even more crazy.'

'Fine,' Flag agreed. 'But what *are* we going to do?'

'It's already done. Was so the minute we killed Sturdevant. Jesus, Ty, we was all crazy with drinkin' that whisky . . . oh, hell, ain't no takin' it back now.'

★　★　★

162

Flag went back down to his table, ignoring the questions from the men at the bar. A couple of minutes later Meers came down and crossed over to speak with the Boxed-C riders.

Ty Flag was going over everything in his mind. Thoughts crowded his mind. Thoughts about the incident at the cabin. Sturdevant's ugly death, which at the time had been like a wild game that had gripped the three of them. He knew now that it had got way out of hand. He and Meers had followed Perry's lead — which was what they always did — and got away with it because of who he was. The drink had got them all in its grip. The thought of the Indian girl had been a prize worth going after. Young and beautiful, far in excess of any of the girls who plied their trade in the saloons in town, she had dominated Perry's thoughts for weeks. None of them had considered the consequences. As far as they were concerned she was just a Ute squaw. There for the taking. And on that day it all seemed to come together. Sturdevant hadn't been at the cabin when they rode in. Inflamed by the whisky they had made their play and it had seemed to be going their way until Sturdevant made an unexpected return.

From that moment it had all gone to hell. Perry had beaten the girl in his drunken fury. Between them they had wrecked the cabin. Had turned on Sturdevant when he came at them. And with his usual twisted humor Perry had doused the man in oil and set him alight. A sheer moment of wanton violence. They had caught up their horses and chased him through the trees . . . and found themselves confronted by the man they now knew as Jess McCall . . . yet when they had tried to subdue him and haul him back to town with the intention of blaming him for Sturdevant's death even that had backfired. McCall had escaped. He had shot Flag and stole his horse. By the time they had returned to Culhane the mess had become even more tangled.

Marshal Teague, never a one to conceal his dislike for Perry, had more or less taken the Texan's side of the story.

Flag downed the glass of whisky in front of him. The liquor burned its way down with more than usual ferocity. It sat heavily in Flag's stomach. He heard laughter from the bar where Meers was drinking with the crew.

What the hell did he have to be so cheerful about?

All it would take now was for that Indian girl — he'd even forgotten her name — to start telling her side of the story. Anger rose in Flag. Anger at their stupidity at letting her get away. Drunk as they were all they could think about was hogtying the Texan and dragging him back to town and she had run off while they were doing that. By the time they had thought about her it was too late. She had gone. Escaping into the wilderness forest. Somewhere she was at home in. Too late to go looking for her. All they could hope was she would stay well away from them.

Now it seemed even that was turning around on them. If she was in the care of the town doctor she might talk enough to point the finger. If she did it would take more than Perry's persuasion to reverse things.

Flag's mind went over and over everything. The way things were going not even Perry's old man would be able to do anything. The Major might be a big man around Culhane, but the one thing he didn't control was the law. John Teague was his own man. Beholden to no one. If he heard the truth from the girl, confirming McCall's story, then everything would blow up in their faces.

He thought then of Ira Begley. Flag had never much liked the man. A toady who worked for Major Culhane and considered himself to be important, which was all in his mind. Begley had always tried to ingratiate himself with Perry and his close friends. His nosiness had led to his death when he picked up loose talk between Meers and Perry and they had taken the opportunity to silence him during the street confrontation between Flag and McCall. It made Flag realize the threat they were all under from anyone with information.

Jesus, what a damned mess.

A wild burst of laughter erupted from the bar. Flag twisted round, his move causing him a fresh burst of pain from his shoulder. He clutched his hand. *Damn that McCall.* Twice now he had put a slug into Flag. The doc had told him he would have to be careful now. If the wounds failed to heal correctly Flag might suffer from a crippled arm. It hadn't been the news Flag wanted to hear.

The pain seemed to increase even as he thought about it. Flag pushed to his feet and walked out of the saloon. The earlier breeze had increased. Dust rattled against the buildings, gritty and harsh. Flag felt it against his pants as he stood on the edge of the boardwalk. He gripped his hat as it threatened to blow away. Across the rutted street he could see the doctor's office. Lamplight showing behind the windows, and one of the upstairs windows where there were patient rooms. He decided to take a walk down there. Maybe the doc could give him something to ease the pain. He needed something. The way it was hurting he wasn't going to get much sleep.

Flag stood at the door. He checked the street, not quite sure why, then opened the door and stepped inside. There didn't appear to be anyone around. The office was deserted. Then he heard the quiet murmur of voices coming from the rear of the building. That would be where the doctor and his wife had their living quarters. To his right a staircase led to the upper floor. Where there were rooms for patients who needed care, he reminded himself.

Like the Indian girl.

Her name came to him then.

Mountain Spirit.

That was it.

Flag allowed a thin smile to curve his

lips. His left hand dropped to the butt of his cross-draw Colt. If he had his way the girl could go join her ancestor spirits. He clamped his lips tight when the smile almost became a giggle. That was the whisky. He hadn't eaten for a while so the intake of liquor was having an effect. He took some deep breaths.

Calm down, boy, and do this quiet.

Do it right and maybe their problems would go away.

He went up the stairs, close to the side, testing each riser before he put his weight on it. He reached the landing without having any creaks betray his presence. Pausing outside the door to the room with the lighted window Flag reached down and turned the knob, gently easing the door free. He pulled his gun. Flag used the toe of his boot to push the door wide, following it quickly.

Whatever he was about to do had to be done fast. If this was where Mountain Spirit was, he needed to finish her without any fuss. He felt the weight of his pistol in his hand. No shooting. The heavy weapon would make an effective club. A couple of solid blows to her head, enough to crack her skull should be enough.

There was a lamp on a small table beside the bed. The illumination showed the covered shape of the girl. Despite the bruising and cuts on her face Flag recognized her. It was Mountain Spirit, her thick black hair standing out against the white pillow her head rested on.

This could turn out to be easier than I figured.

Flag moved into the room.

In his eagerness to carry out his threat he failed to notice the still figure in the cane chair in the gloom beyond the throw of the lamplight. Failed until the figure moved, pushing to his feet.

It was Joe Crown.

And he was taking in the armed man moving towards Mountain Spirit's bed.

He saw the lamplight glint on the pistol in Flag's hand. Crown saw the weapon half-risen. Saw, too, the anger on Flag's burned face.

'*Hey,*' Crown said, and saw Flag turn at the sound of his voice. 'Put it down, you son of a bitch.'

Flag's gun began to drop, the muzzle turning in at Crown.

There was no hesitation in Crown's response. His right hand dipped and when it rose again he was holding his .45 caliber Colt, the hammer already back. The boom of the shot was loud in the confines of the room. It was followed by a second shot, both slugs thudding into Flag's chest. Flag stepped back, his mouth dropping open. He stumbled and fell to his knees, staring at Crown as if he couldn't believe what had just happened. He found he couldn't breathe easily any more and there was numbness engulfing his body. The warm taste of blood rising in his throat. When he dropped to the floor he was already close to death. Both of Crown's slugs had taken him in the heart. His hand let go of his gun and it bounced across the carpet as his fingers splayed apart.

Crown moved around the bed. He

cleared Flag's dropped weapon, then went to see if Mountain Spirit was safe. When he leaned over the bed he saw her eyes were open and she was staring up him.

'It's over,' Crown said. 'You're safe now.'

Her gaze fixed on him. Unblinking. Searching his face.

'They have killed Sturdevant,' she said. 'He is gone.'

'No easy way to say it, girl, but yeah, he's gone.'

The doctor and his wife burst into the room. Marian came directly to the bed.

'She's fine,' Crown said. He realized he still had his gun in his hand and quickly put it away. He glanced at Cavanaugh. 'You know him?'

The doctor said he did. 'Ty Flag. One of Perry Culhane's little group.'

Crown indicated the gun Flag had dropped. 'Visitors usually bring flowers,' he said.

'My God, do you think he was going

to hurt Mountain Spirit?' Marian said.

'Ma'am, I don't have to think. If I hadn't been here you would have just lost your patient.'

Mountain Spirit pushed herself slowly into a sitting position, ignoring the discomfort. Marian held her. Mountain Spirit leaned over so she could look down at Flag. She took a long look at him, her face expressionless.

'You recognize him?' Marian asked.

The girl nodded slowly.

'Even with his marked face I recognize him. He is Flag. He came to our cabin with Meers and Perry Culhane. They were the ones who set Sturdevant on fire and killed him. Sturdevant said I should always be truthful and never hide from things.' She looked across at Crown. 'You saved me from Flag. This I will never forget, Joe Crown.'

'I believe we need to have Marshal Teague hear what you have to say, young lady,' Marian Cavanaugh said as she helped Mountain Spirit lie down again. 'You should go and fetch him, Joe.'

Crown stood over the girl, concern on his face. 'She going to be all right?'

Mountain Spirit's free hand reached out and she took hold of Crown's arm. 'I am safe here now. Go and bring whoever you need, Joe Crown. There is no need for you to be concerned.'

After Crown had left Marian Cavanaugh said, 'He will be concerned for her no matter what.'

The doctor smiled. 'No matter what,' he agreed.

15

Major Culhane arrived in town with dawn streaking the sky. He rode in with only one man with him. Culhane was astride his favorite horse, a powerful, splendid looking chestnut mare. As befitting an ex-military man the Major sat upright in his saddle, controlling the chestnut with strong hands. He looked neither left or right as he took his horse along the street, ignoring the gusting wind that had remained since the previous night. He drew rein outside the jail, dismounted and passed the reins to one of his men.

'Cole, would you go and find out where my . . . where Perry is. At a guess he'll be in *The Golden Deuce*.'

Cole Landers, a lean man, wearing range clothes and carrying a holstered Remington .44 caliber revolver, turned his horse along the street.

'I need to talk with the marshal,' Culhane said as Landers moved away.

He stepped up on the boardwalk and walked into the jail.

'Teague, we need to discuss this matter,' he said without any kind of preamble.

Teague was behind his desk, holding a hot coffee in his hands.

He had sent Mort home earlier. The only other person in the office was Seth Tyler, seated across from the town marshal.

'Major, we certainly do.'

'This nonsense about Perry and his men.'

Teague placed his mug on the desk, glancing at Seth briefly before picking up sheets of paper. He held up the documents.

'This is a sworn statement given by a witness who was present when Carl Sturdevant was attacked, doused in coal oil and set on fire. Said witness, who was also attacked, identified the men involved as Perry Culhane, Buck Meers and Ty Flag. The statement was witnessed and signed by Seth Tyler here. He's the marshal from the town of Hope.' The marshal of Culhane paused. 'You were going to say, Major?'

Culhane reached out and took the documents. An uneasy silence descended as he slowly read through the statement. His face grew pale as he did so. After some time he lowered the papers and stared across the desk at Teague.

'Who is this Mountain Spirit?'

'A Ute Indian who lived with Carl Sturdevant. And before you ask, Major, we consider her to be a competent witness. She speaks and understands English well enough. It seems Sturdevant taught her. She's an intelligent young woman. As far as I'm concerned she has given us an honest account of what happened.'

'But she's an . . . '

Seth cleared his throat. 'Major Culhane, I hope you're not going to tell us because she's an Indian her words are not to be accepted. Right now that wouldn't be very wise.'

'Yes, you're right. I apologize for what I said.'

'You should also know, Major,' Teague said, 'that last night, Ty Flag made an attempt to attack the young woman at the doc's. If it hadn't been for one of Marshal Tyler's friends who was watching over her, Flag might have succeeded. Flag is dead. Mountain Spirit even identified him as one of the three men who attacked her and murdered Sturdevant.'

Culhane sank into an empty chair, silenced now, because there was no denying what he had heard.

'Sorry to have to tell you these things, Major, but there's no doubt now that it was Perry and his friends who carried out the events in that statement. I have to tell you there's no way he can walk away from it. Ira Begley was murdered last night. Knifed to death in an alley. No proof as such yet but I have a feeling his death is a result of Perry's crimes.'

'I feel responsible,' the Major said.

'For Perry's actions. Too many times I've given in to his indiscretions. Allowed him to get away with . . . ' he hesitated, ' . . . I almost said *murder*. It seems as if this time that's what it is. Murder. To top off all the other things my son has done he's now killed someone simply to conceal his actions.'

Culhane fell silent, his eyes staring beyond Teague but not really seeing anything. The moment dragged because what needed saying would come hard.

'I'm going to have to arrest Perry and Meers,' Teague said. 'No other choice, Major.'

'Yes . . . I understand,' Culhane said in a quiet tone. He stood. 'I have things to do.'

He left the office then, closing the door behind him. Watching through the window Seth saw the man mount his horse and move off up the street.

'That was a moment I could have done without,' Teague said. 'And so is what I got to do next.'

When Seth didn't answer Teague

looked round. Seth was on his feet, crossing to stare out the window.

'Something wrong?'

'Not sure,' Seth told him.

They both heard the approaching sound of a train whistle.

'That'll be the one with McCall's friend on board,' Teague said.

Seth had taken out his pistol. He checked it was fully loaded before he slid it back into the holster.

'Way you did that makes me think you might need it,' Teague said.

'Something's telling me I just might.'

Seth was not wrong.

16

8.26 a.m.

Jess McCall left the hotel and turned towards the rail depot. He could see smoke rising above the rooftops as the train slowed in its approach. He felt the morning breeze against his face and snugged his new hat down. As he crossed the street he saw Major Culhane reining his horse outside *The Golden Deuce* saloon and decided it was early for someone like him to be going for a drink. McCall figured it was none of his business actually, so he continued across the street.

The train slid into the station as McCall approached the platform.

8.27 a.m.

'Just lend me your firearm,' Major Culhane said.

Landers, the man he had sent to check the place, had already informed him Perry was inside. Now he stood facing his employer, unsure what was happening.

'Cole, please.' Culhane held out his hand. 'Good Lord, man, I only want to borrow it.'

Landers slid his pistol from leather and handed it over. It was the .44 Remington Single Action the man always carried. A nicely maintained, well-balanced weapon. The Major checked it. Spun the cylinder. Weighed the weapon as if he was familiarizing himself with it.

'Thank you,' he said.

'You sure about this, sir?'

Culhane smiled. 'Oh, yes,' he said. 'Very sure.'

He stepped up on the boardwalk and hesitated at the saloon entrance. Took a breath, then pushed his way inside through the batwings.

<u>8.28 a.m.</u>
'Damned if he isn't going in,' Seth said as he and Teague made their way up the street.

They increased their pace, both aware that they could easily be too late and both of them drew their weapons.

The distance suddenly seemed longer than it was.

<u>8.29 a.m.</u>
Culhane had paused as he went into the saloon, his gaze taking in the few men at the bar before settling on the men he had come to find.

'You need to come with me. Both of you,' he said.

Major Culhane stood just inside the saloon door, facing across the room. His attention was focused on the table where Perry and Buck Meers sat. He ignored the men at the bar. Some of them worked for him and they stood in awkward silence. Perry and Meers were both facing in his direction. On the

183

table were breakfast plates. Mugs of coffee.

'If you've come for breakfast, Major,' Meers said, a crooked grin on his face, 'you're too damn late.'

It was then that Culhane noticed the near empty whisky bottle on the table and the glass in his son's hand.

'Hell of a thing,' Perry said. 'I never would have known whisky and bacon went together.'

His hair was tousled and his clothes looked as if he had slept in them. He needed a shave and there were dark circles under his eyes. Culhane noticed that Perry's handgun lay on the table close to his right hand.

'Sorry, *Father*, were you saying something?' He gave a soft giggle.

Buck Meers shifted in his chair. The expression in his eyes was cold, penetrating. There was no hint of any respect as he faced his employer.

'Something about we needing to go with him,' he said.

'Perry, it's finished,' Culhane said.

'The Indian girl who was with Sturde-vant has identified you and your friends as the men who killed him.'

'That damn squaw? Who's going to take her word?'

'The marshal has a signed statement from her. Her story matches up to what that that Texan, McCall, said. Flag tried to kill her last night but it was him who died.'

'The hell with all of them,' Perry said. He swept his arm across the table, knocking objects out of the way. 'Damn this town,' he yelled. 'Oh, I forgot, *your* town, Major goddamn Culhane.'

Culhane took a step forward, the borrowed gun in his hand covering Perry and Meers.

'No more, Perry. You've taken things too far this time. I can't allow you to . . . '

His words were drowned by the crash of gunshots as Perry snatched up the pistol sitting next to him, lined it up and put two slugs into his father.

'*You won't allow? You?* The hell

with you, old man. No more demands. I've had enough of your damned orders. Time for me to make my own decisions.'

As Culhane stumbled back, his son's slugs in his chest, Perry and Meers kicked back their chairs and headed for the exit. They had rifles leaning against the side of their table and picked them up as they headed for the door. Major Culhane was half-sitting, his back to the wall as they passed him, blood soaking through his shirt. Perry didn't even look down at him.

Landers was halfway up the steps to the boardwalk. He had taken his Winchester from the saddle boot and was working the lever. He took a .44-40 slug in the shoulder as Meers threw up his own rifle and fired from no more than five feet away. Keller lurched back, stumbling off the steps and slamming to the ground.

Perry and Meers stood on the boardwalk, eyes scanning the street. The few people in sight were already backing away.

Except Teague and Seth Tyler who

were moving towards them, wind whipped dust tugging at their clothes.

'Here's the law,' Meers said and raised his rifle. 'This could turn out to be a good day after all.'

8.31 a.m.

'Can't let you out of my sight for you to get into some kind of scrape,' Chet Ballard said as he stepped from the train. His saddle was carried against his left hip and he wore his holstered Colt under the jacket of his dark suit.

'Nice to see you too, son,' McCall told him.

'New hat?' Ballard said.

'Kind of lost the other when I had to jump in a creek.'

'Let you tell me about that later.'

As they moved across the platform, bypassing the station office, McCall said, 'I'll tell you the whole sorry story over a cup of . . . '

Gunshots echoed in the crisp morning air.

'Nice quiet town,' Ballard observed.

'Has its moments,' McCall said.

They cleared the boardwalk . . .

*　　*　　*

Across the street Perry Culhane and Buck Meers were moving apart. They were both raising their rifles and arcing them round to pick targets.

'McCall,' Meers yelled to Perry as he spotted the Texan.

'He's mine,' Perry said.

'Lawdogs,' Meers growled, swinging his rifle in towards Teague and Seth Tyler. 'Don't like lawdogs.'

He triggered fast shots that fell short. Meers cursed himself for being too eager and stepped forward, taking steadier aim. He got off one more shot, the slug hitting Teague in the left arm and throwing his aim. Meers saw his chance and levered another round into the breech. He didn't make it. Seth, pausing and turning sideways on, raised his pistol and triggered a single shot, the .45 caliber slug taking Meers in the torso. The impact stopped Meers in his tracks, indecision ghosting across his face. Before the racket of Seth's shot had faded the Hope lawman fired a second shot, his aim perfect, and the heavy lead slug hit Meers above his left eye. It jerked his head back as it cored in through his skull and blew out a chunk of bone in a gout of bloody debris. This time Meers stiffened and toppled onto his back.

★ ★ ★

Before Meers struck the ground Perry had taken steps across the street, dropping his rifle and letting his hand hover over his holstered pistol. All his building frustration was gathering in his mind and he saw McCall as being the one who was behind it all.

'McCall,' he said. 'Damn your eyes, mister, this is all down to you. No way you can walk away from me this time.'

'Son, I ain't moving,' McCall answered.

'Seein' as how you made my life hell from the minute I was unlucky enough meet up with you, I figure *I* got just as much to gripe about as well you.'

'You talk to much, McCall.'

'Never been accused of that before. So what are you waiting for, son? Play your hand if you figure you have to.'

McCall saw Perry's hand curve in towards the butt of his Colt, shoulders hunching slightly as he set himself. He was showing all the signs of getting set to draw his gun.

A flickering image raised itself in McCall's mind. Only for a fragment of a second.

It was of a burning man. Writhing, falling, encased in flame that seared his flesh and McCall was sure he could hear those terrible sounds — the tortured scream filling his ears again.

And as Perry's hand gripped his pistol and lifted it clear, the muzzle starting to line up in a blur, McCall drew his own weapon, trigger held back so when he worked the hammer with his left hand the roll of shots merged into one long burst of thunder. He put all five shots into Perry Culhane, the .45 lead slugs tearing into his chest and slapping him to the street. McCall's pistol was back in his holster before Perry hit the ground and died.

'I get the feeling you really meant that,' Ballard said.

'Hell, son, I had to get it out of my system. And it was just what that little pissant needed.'

Seth was walking towards them, Teague gripping his blood-soaked arm as they headed for the doctor's office.

'If I say it myself,' Teague murmured, 'it's a hell of a way to start the day.'

It was something they could all agree on.

★ ★ ★

The Major didn't die. He took a time recovering after Cavanaugh removed the bullets from his chest. Any grieving he might have held for his son was done privately. As soon as he was able he gathered his crew around him and held Boxed-C together. It was a slow process, helped by the townspeople who showed considerable strength. Cole Landers took over the responsibility of the ranch fully until his employer was strong enough to step up and take control again.

Marshal John Teague and his deputy Mort Pickett had no complaints when Culhane reverted back to its previous predictable existence. In truth they were content the whole affair was over. Some time later Teague made the trip back to the hillside cabin and made sure Carl Sturdevant received a decent burial. Mountain Spirit made the ride with him to say her own farewell, along with Joe Crown who had stayed behind to help her, stating he would return to Hope when Mountain Spirit was ready. The tough, often taciturn cowboy, had found someone in the determined Indian girl he refused to walk away from. And it was evident from the way she clung to Crown both physically and spiritually that she felt the same. When he told her he wanted her to return with him to the Tyler ranch Mountain Spirit's reply was an instant yes.

Jess McCall and Chet Ballard, along with Seth Tyler and Lew Riley, eventually headed out across the mountain to Hope to complete the purchase of the breeding cattle McCall had first come to Colorado for. With Culhane behind them and the slow ride ahead, McCall said his final words on what had happened.

'Chet, if I ever go on a rail trip again and the train breaks down . . . well, hell, son, this boy won't budge. I'll sit there and wait for them to fix it. Long as it takes, or Hell freezes over . . . '

BALLARD & MCCALL:
TWO FROM TEXAS
GUNS OF THE BRASADA

We do hope that you have enjoyed reading this large print book.

Did you know that all of our titles are available for purchase?

We publish a wide range of high quality large print books including:
Romances, Mysteries, Classics
General Fiction
Non Fiction and Westerns

Special interest titles available in large print are:
The Little Oxford Dictionary
Music Book, Song Book
Hymn Book, Service Book

Also available from us courtesy of Oxford University Press:
Young Readers' Dictionary
(large print edition)
Young Readers' Thesaurus
(large print edition)

For further information or a free brochure, please contact us at:
Ulverscroft Large Print Books Ltd.,
The Green, Bradgate Road, Anstey,
Leicester, LE7 7FU, England.
Tel: (00 44) **0116 236 4325**
Fax: (00 44) **0116 234 0205**

THE OUTLAW TRAIL

Paul Bedford

Along the infamous Outlaw Trail, three parties' paths will cross — with unforeseen consequences. Former lawman Rance Toller and his companion Angie Sutter are heading south to the warmer climes of Arizona. Cole Hastings, a vicious rustler, has amassed a huge herd of stolen horses intended for sale to the US Army in Arizona. And dogging his footsteps is Chad Seevers, who not only wants his herd back, but also seeks revenge for a murder . . .

McANDREW'S STAND

Bill Cartright

Jenny McAndrew and her two sons live in the valley known as McAndrew's Pass. When they hear that the new Rocky Mountains Railroad Company has plans to lay a line through the valley — and their farm — they are devastated at the prospect of their simple lives being destroyed. Clarence Harper, the ruthless boss of the railroad company, is not a man to brook opposition. But in the McAndrews, he finds one family that will not be bullied into submission . . .

THE ROBIN HOOD OF THE RANGE

James Clay

Ricky Cates is a vicious outlaw who kills without remorse. He also has a talent for deception, having convinced a local writer that he's the Robin Hood of the Range: a man who takes from the rich and gives to the poor. Rance Dehner is on Cates's blood-spattered trail. But before he can reach his target, he must confront Cates's henchmen, another detective obsessed with catching the killer — and a young woman who is hopelessly and dangerously in love with this Robin Hood . . .

BITTER CREEK RANCH

Saran Essex

Now owners of the Bitter Creek Ranch in Wyoming, Butch Cassidy and The Sundance Kid have swapped robbing banks and trains for a more relaxed pace of life. Or so they think . . . For when sisters Rosa and Louisa Jordan come to the ranch, trouble quickly follows in the form of their stepbrother Abe Gannon. The violent outlaw is tired of living in the shadow of Butch and Sundance, and wants to teach them a lesson . . .

A NOOSE FOR IRON EYES

Rory Black

The infamous bounty hunter Iron Eyes is on the trail of a pair of lawman-killers, following them into the Black Hills. But as the pursuit moves deeper into the forest, other enemies materialise — for this is Sioux territory, and they do not take kindly to intruders. However, his dogged companion Squirrel Sally is well aware of Iron Eyes' penchant for getting himself into sticky situations, and is not far behind him . . .

HOOFBEATS WEST

Colin Bainbridge

When Jess Caird, owner of the White Sage, finds one of his cowhands murdered and a barn set on fire, he sets out with old-timer Horner to bring the culprit to justice. Evidence points to Caleb Grote, a notorious gunslinger, and the trail leads to the settlement of Sand Ridge. There, Caird encounters businessman Dugmore, head of the local Pony Express which employs Caird's nephew. Is there a connection between Dugmore and Grote . . . ?